CW01301287

'Pellucid clinical sentences craft a loving symphony of meat and magic, mucous, mud and mire. Cynan Jones's writing is pure electric energy. It slows time, changes the pace of perception somehow, pulls your guts out and stitches them back in with gentle veterinarian precision, strength and surety. Every story thrums and squirms with life. The cumulative effect is to deliver a shock to the heart of what a wild, strange and wonderful thing it is to be human'   Megan Barker

'Breathtakingly tense, vital and precise. Cynan Jones has a rare gift for making us experience, moment by moment, the struggles of his characters to survive'   Carys Davies

'Reading these stories, I'm reminded of what was once said about Emily Dickinson, that it ought to be impossible to cram so much meaning into so few words. Each paragraph reads like a beautiful, multi-layered prose poem. The crystalline language conveys, with real emotive power, the squelch and suck of mud and manure, the stink of blood, the skin-feel of drizzle. Spending time with this collection is a sensory, immersive experience. This is what writing can, and ought to, do' Niall Griffiths

'Jones's prose is extraordinary, somehow managing to be simultaneously rich and spare. Each of the stories is a novel in miniature, a whole emotional landscape evoked precisely with the most minimal gestures'   Jessie Greengrass

'These are stories of elemental power, which dramatise the collision of external and internal forces to thrilling and unsettling effect. Their exploration of the struggle between people and nature – both that of the world, and their own – is always riveting and frequently heartbreaking. *Pulse* is a magnificent collection'   James Scudamore

'These six stories of characters in states of extreme jeopardy are rendered in language of relentless and precise power and the overall effect is of an almost visionary intensity. *Pulse* is a remarkable collection from a writer of singular gifts'   Tom Lee

'*Pulse* reveals the bloody, brutal and beautiful truth of rural life. Hewn with a sparse, poetic vision, it offers an unflinching, visceral account of the often neglected lives of those who toil the land. There is no finer nature writer than Cynan Jones'   Adelle Stripe

'A master of concision and precision, Cynan Jones crafts stories as taut as steel wire, a tightrope display of careful draughtsmanship and daring language. Seemingly taking their cue from the collection's title, these often intense tales veritably pulse with life and a verbal vitality as suddenly charged as a quick intake of breath'   Jon Gower

PULSE

Also by Cynan Jones:

The Long Dry
Everything I Found on the Beach
Bird, Blood, Snow
The Dig
Cove
Three Tales
Stillicide

Pulse

Cynan Jones

GRANTA

Granta Publications, 12 Addison Avenue, London W11 4QR

First published in Great Britain by Granta Books, 2025

Copyright © 2025 Cynan Jones

Cynan Jones has asserted his moral right under the Copyright, Designs and Patents Act, 1988, to be identified as the author of this work.

'Peregrine' first broadcast by BBC Radio 4 (2024), 'White Squares' first broadcast by BBC Radio 4 (2018), 'Reindeer' first published by Hingston & Olsen Publishing (2022), 'Cow' first appeared in *Freeman's Animals* (Grove Atlantic, 2022), 'Stock', commissioned as a creative response to the work of the Narrating Rural Change network, first published by Nightjar Press (2023) and in *Best British Short Stories* (Salt, 2024), and 'Pulse' first published in the *New Yorker* (2024).

All rights reserved. This book is copyright material and must not be copied, reproduced, transferred, distributed, leased, licensed or publicly performed or used in any way except as specifically permitted in writing by the publisher, as allowed under the terms and conditions under which it was purchased or as strictly permitted by applicable copyright law. Any unauthorised distribution or use of this text may be a direct infringement of the author's and publisher's rights, and those responsible may be liable in law accordingly. Please note that no part of this book may be used or reproduced in any manner for the purpose of training artificial intelligence technologies or systems.

A CIP catalogue record for this book is available from the British Library.

1 3 5 7 9 10 8 6 4 2

ISBN 978 1 78378 277 2 (hardback)
ISBN 978 1 78378 278 9 (ebook)

Typeset in Warnock by Patty Rennie

Printed and bound by CPI Group (UK) Ltd, Croydon, CR0 4YY

www.granta.com

The manufacturer's authorised representative in the EU for product safety is Authorised Rep Compliance Ltd, 71 Lower Baggot Street, Dublin D02 P593 Ireland (arccompliance.com)

MIX
Paper | Supporting responsible forestry
FSC® C013604

x.

Contents

PEREGRINE 1

REINDEER 13

COW 49

STOCK 93

WHITE SQUARES 135

PULSE 143

Peregrine

WHEN THE FORM of the two men appeared, the birds, luminous somehow in the night's moon, lifted from the shallow water where the river met the sea. The men came onto the beach, set the pack down on the stones, then the bigger man went back for the motor.

There was a blue, deep quality to the moon's light and the white edge of the sea looked powdery. Where it broke was like the edge of torn paper. It made just a gentle rattle of sound.

While the bigger man was gone, the lean man undid the straps of the pack, laid out the inflatable boat, and began to pump it up. He looked like some nervous wading animal, made even leaner by the wetsuit he wore, standing on one leg, his other leg lifting and pressing on the pump. The wetsuit was stickled with dun grey terrier hairs as if it attracted them.

When the bigger man returned, carrying the motor on his shoulder, the gulls lifted again and this time went away to the other side of the river.

When the boat was inflated, they carried it out to the water.

The larger man sat in the boat and received the rucksack and coats, and the fishing rods they'd brought in case they were seen; then the lean man went in up to his waist to drag the boat out.

The cold struck through his wetsuit.

As he went back for the outboard, the dog hair caught the moonlight so that parts of the suit seemed woven with filament.

Together the two men fitted the motor over the transom and, with it tipped so as not to catch in the shallows, tightened the clamps. Then the lean man got awkwardly in.

With the added weight the boat sank somewhat against the submerged rocks and the heavier man used the short paddle to push and scud the boat into the calm water past the breakers.

When they were clear, he lowered the motor. Gave the starter cord three hard tugs.

The sudden noise as the motor kicked alive subdued immediately when he backed off the revs. The motor spat a little, gurgled, then he headed the boat out.

The moon sat in the churned wake behind the boat. The light in the disturbed surface seemed to come from the water itself, the way colour comes to dug-up earth.

The gulls against the cliff appeared to hold the same contained potential, wax-like, for light, dropping now and then from the dark face and wheeling out at the sound of the boat. This brought some whelm into the lean man's centre. An uneasy qualm.

With an inward push of anger against that, he took the rucksack from under the coats and brought out a strange harness; still sat, he stepped into it and manoeuvred it to the tops of his legs. He slipped the harness over his arms and buckled it at the chest, then tightened it, adjusted the various straps, all the while half sitting.

A gooseskin came on the backs of his hands, and he told himself it was from the cool air of the moving boat. But as he looked at the face of the cliffs, he could not stop the thought that the boy was somewhere up there, watching, still sitting there.

*

When he'd gone to fix the rope, that afternoon, there he'd been. Sat. Inexplicably, on the clifftop, the boy. Engrossed. Sat bent over himself as if kicked in the stomach.

The lean man had hesitated on the path, stilled and hushed the terrier. Stood, the rotted marine smell from the gulls' nest on the cliff face below lifting in the warm afternoon sun.

The boy reminded the lean man of a boy he'd bullied at school, had a notebook held open on his lap, as if he held the spread wing of a pale bird to count the feathers. And for a horrible moment the lean man thought, it is him. It is actually *that* boy.

When the boy turned his head, the lean man ducked out of sight behind the bracken, saw the cuckoo spit on the campions that pinked the bank.

His gob of spittle, hung, stretched, the kid's flushed skin.

The tribal drumming of the straps on the school bus roof as he held the rucksack out of the skylight. How it had ballooned away into the air.

His own rucksack, as he crouched, heavy with the coiled rope and the lead pad to hold the lines submerged. The strange globe of the small float he'd attach on the fetch line, hung off the rucksack, an eye-shaped shadow on the ground beside him.

A frustrated whine left the terrier.

A formation of gulls slid along the thermal of the cliff.

It wasn't my fault. It wasn't my fault what happened to the boy. I wasn't the only one. The boy did that to himself.

As the bright gulls went past, one of them, needlessly, it seemed, tucked in a wing and for a moment rolled sideways in the sky; and in that moment the unnerve had pulsed into the man, as if he had lost his own footing.

It's not him. It can't be.

But he had looked so similar. To *that* boy. All those years ago.

*

The two men had come in under the dark shadow of the cliff now, the motor idling, the putter knocking back off the rockface; the slush of water lapped.

Every so often the inflatable bounced subtly on the great rocks that even in the high tide were only just below the water. The boat less rigid without momentum.

The leaner man reached and hooked the small float with the paddle and drew it in. He unknotted the float and put it in the floor of the boat with a hollow pat; then he unfolded the pad of lead that had kept the two ends of the rope in the water since the afternoon. Next, he knotted the two ends of the rope loosely to the gunwale cord and looked along the rope that travelled away and seemed to disappear against the nightshade of the rock.

He could sense the bigger man watch the boat's position. The engine tick, chok. The short remnant of security chain clinked against the casing.

The nervousness seemed to expand in the lean man and he shook slightly. Again, he told himself it was the cold.

The boy being there. It doesn't mean anything. *The way the one gull had purposelessly tumbled.* It's the chill. It's just the chill getting to you.

The big man by now used the short paddle to help keep the craft a few yards out from the base of the cliff and the lean man was about to speak, to tell the bigger man about the boy and the gull, but then he looked up at the solid cliff, at the reality of it, and knew he was in it now, there was no way out.

The hairs on the wetsuit looked then like they could have come from the bigger man's beard. As if he'd been snuffled by him. Little dog. That's what the bigger man had taken to calling him, after hearing him use that way of speaking to the terrier. Come on, little dog, the bigger man would say.

The lean man put on the wetsuit hood. He looked like a frogman. Then he put on the builders' boots.

He took the one thick leather glove and the canvas drawstring bag from the rucksack and stuffed them in under his harness. Clicked the head torch on–off briefly then fitted it over his head. Put the safety goggles on.

When he tugged the knot to check the rope was fast to the D-ring attached to his harness, the shake through him thickened as if he'd pulled at his core. He felt the boy was on the cliff, and that it was he who held the rope.

The bigger man put the paddle down, undid the end of the rope left tied to the gunwale cord and secured it to a ring on his own belt. He gave the smaller man a look. Like he *was* some little dog. Then the smaller man switched on the head torch and stood balancing up in the front of the boat.

The swell took them in, and when the bow bumped at the base of the cliff the lean man felt urgently for a hold and, gripping hard so the shake went out of his hand, stepped out of the boat, scrabbled with his feet to find purchase.

For that moment he felt he had stepped into nothingness. Hung, one foot loose, the water soaking through his boot, every inch shaking against the face of the shale. Then he felt the motor rev, water bubble, those sounds seeming to come from the rock itself. As if there were some deep activity within.

The feel of the rope as it taughtened was the weird lurch of going over a humpback. It pulled him off the cliff and he felt sick, grabbed out. The head torch cracked plasticly as he swung back and bounced unforcefully into the cliff, the impact wetsuit-cushioned; then he got control of himself. The rope had him. That's all he had to tell himself.

The boy doesn't mean anything. It's nothing. It wasn't *that* boy.

He tried to help his weight up the cliff, but in reality he was just being winched as the boat drove out and the bigger man pulled on the line, hand over hand.

The scars and curls in the rock seemed mobile in the torchlight. Fingerholds that scuttled off as he reached to find them.

Cold gripless flanks of smoother rock.

Spills of shale that crumbled at his touch.

A few feet below the nest he found an outcrop and stood, balanced, his back to the cliff, the gurn of the boat motor below and all the horrible vertigo of the dark and the expanse and the drop.

Tried to focus through his fear to the peregrine chicks, born onto the bare ledge, the fortune they were worth. Just an arm's reach. Just an arm's reach now.

Then he heard the parent falcons. Their talons scratch on the rock, a low uncertain *chucking* from their throats.

A tremor emptied his limbs. He wanted the rope. Only the rope. Could not marshal his body. He tried to work his hand into the thick leather glove but his body had drained of strength. And as he clutched the rope, wanted it over now, he felt the slack in it. A liquid slack.

High above, in the beam of the head torch, he saw the rope was jammed into a small fissure, as if the rock had taken it in a bite.

He pulled. Uselessly. As the boat motor called out in a futile yowl, the line that travelled out to sea began to moan with strain. With white fear he pulled again.

And the world gave way. Fell from him. The overhang dislodged. With deafening volleys of rock careened off the cliff, splinters into the sea beneath. His body *the rucksack ballooning in the air, a swallowed sob*, leg smacked against an outcrop with a crack through his whole body, dangled. Hung facedown, his flailing hands, trying to fly himself to the breakable cliff, swing, with the detonations of his heart hollowing him out, implosions of air.

And they came off the nest. Then. Off they came, screeched and wheeled. Dark stone, shards animate. Keened and batted into him.

Head torch cracked so that its crazed face threw a shadow, an inverse fork of dark lightning that looked like a fracture in the cliff towards which he swung, a dark maw through which he would disappear.

The rope of spittle. Hung scrunched and flinching.

Uselessly flapping as the birds came.

And even in this, though he knew, though he knew, he truly felt the boy was holding the rope. And that was more frightening than anything.

Then there was sudden respite. The falcons braced into the black sky. Headed from the cliff, from the lean man hung there, *kekking* and crying with grief. As if beseeching the world. Not for this to happen. Do not let this happen. Let our children be.

Reindeer

STON PULLED UP the last line and it too had fish. It had two decent fish, and a small fish about which he thought, If I still had the dog I would give it to the dog.

He clubbed the fish with the steel hitch pin from the motor sled and lay them in line with the others on the snow.

Snow had crusted around his knees but his body heat had melted it off the actual knee. The snow on him looked like tight wool.

Ston looked over the flat frozen lake to the white severe mountains. The sky was white too. A white hem of mist hung above and through the black trees beyond which the mountains became truly high.

It was the back edge of real winter.

*

As the police chief neared Ston's cabin he disbelievingly thought a flock of bats hung roosted under the stoop. Then he saw the fresher fish splayed out flatly on the wire, hung in the dun smoke that came up from a bed of embers a little way from the building.

There was no wind and the smoke went straight up and eventually away and the chief did not smell it when he stepped from the 4×4.

Ston, by then, was on the stoop.

*

Ston looked at the box of heavy cartridges.

— Why can't one of you do it?

He picked the box from the table. His hands smelled of the surprise thyme smell specific to the fish, and of the deciduous smoke. His clothes smelled of smoke.

— There's only three of us, and they've put Jonanssen down to part-time. And you know what it's like, this time of year. Besides. They wouldn't be much good at it.

— Then, you go.

— Right.

Ston fingered the sharp tips of the cartridges and the space where one was missing. The stamp of sale was still on the box with his name on and the number of his gun licence. The paint was lifted in a centimetre-thick line that still had red flakes of the evidence tape the police chief had removed.

— Will you do it?

Ston stood from the table and reached a bottle from the cupboard over the kettle.

— Drink?

— No, Ston. I don't want a drink. You know I don't.

— Ah. Well.

The high clean chemical smell came out of the glass as Ston poured for himself.

— Bears should be asleep now.

— This one isn't.

*

— Don't shoot anything but the bear.

— I'll have to eat.

Even though he knew they were fish, the police chief still thought the smoked fish on the stoop were bats. Close up they were not soot-coloured but the subdued golden of the bullet casings.

— Can I shoot something to draw the bear in?

— Don't shoot anything that's on a list. And don't shoot farm stock.

— Aren't the stock still in?

— Mostly. I guess that's why the bear's come down.

There was a rich brownness now in the smoke that lifted off the trench of embers. The edge of the embers glowed occasionally when a barest ground-level breeze went over them. There were the heavy alder poles to hold the wire and the split bat-shaped fish hung up to smoke, turning from silver-grey to soft brass. Other fish lay in a tray of salt on the stoop rail, their skins tightening.

In the salt it looked like they lay again in the snow. Their eyes had gone milky.

Out beyond the cabin were the great hills and snow and the steam lifting off the plantation leaves. Everything was clean white but the black angular forests.

— She's holding, this year.

— Yep.

— They're saying high up the sun melts it then it goes back to ice over and over. The animals can't get down to the grass.

The police chief saw Ston look up to the slopes. Took in the winter isolation of the cabin.

— You know you can come back in?

— No.

— Ston.

— Not with what people think. I'll need fuel. Maybe a radio.

— We'll cover it.

— I'll get up high, Ston said. I'll get up, then I'll be able to watch. Hopefully that will show me where he is. Where he's coming from.

The chief nodded and moved off the stoop.

— Will my sister cook you a fish?

— Not if she knows you sent it.

Ston looked at the bright colourful 4×4.

— Tell her you ran it over.

*

Ston cut the cords that held in place the laundry crate in which the dog used to ride. The nylon, compacted into itself after so long, frayed strand by strand, so that at one point the ends of the cord looked like a thistle flower gone to seed.

In the crate's place, Ston bungee-strapped his tent and the pack with the stove and the flares and other things he'd need or might need. Over this, he stretched the snow cover. He had the shovel and the snowshoes lashed to the sled and the extra jerrycan of fuel secured to the bolts above the runners. He slung the cased rifle on his back.

Partway into his mental checklist he stopped looking at the hump of snow cover as if he could see through it to all the stuff he mentally checked off, went inside and came back with a full bottle. He put it in under the cover, in his pack.

Once he set off, the noise of the motor sled made it impossible to think of anything much else but driving the motor sled.

*

The landscape regained its vastness when he cut the engine before the ground got too steep. With the gradient rising sharply, the trees loomed.

Below Ston was the giant white plateau and across it the powdery line of his route, thrown out like the wake of a boat.

The roofs of the small farmhouses and farm buildings looked toy from this distance. Through the heavy 16×50s he could see the dark dots of fence posts that marked the pens, the snow stained with feed, and the dun puffs of the animals that were not yet put out of the winter fields.

There was no true sunshine. There was no gleam in the snow, but the lateness of the left daylight put a cold faint blue through the slopes.

Ston tethered the motor sled beneath one of the huge larches. The larch still held brass and yellow needles and stood out against the firs. He unloaded his pack, the snowshoes. Then he covered the sled again with the snow cover and set the glaring orange marker flag up in the tree.

He shouldered his pack and the rifle.

It's a long time since you walked properly, he thought. You're not fit.

Anyway, he went up.

*

In the firelight, the world was only the immediate trees and the circle within the firelight. Beyond was a thumping blackness.

The rough trunks looked stony, and as if veins of mineral were through them where the light caught the burst nodes of resin.

Here, in the centre of the forest, the snow had not penetrated completely through the closed canopy. There were occasional bare patches of earth.

The fire spat and clicked quietly, and the soil paled on the nearby ground as the dampness warmed out.

Ston chewed the dried meat. With the third or fourth chew the flavour came. It was dry enough not to have a smell. Nothing the bear could scent.

There was the peppery ironish juice of the chewed meat and the juniper tang of the drink that seemed exaggerated by the conifers.

Later, as he lay in the tent, Ston felt the strange abstract understanding fear, and the mantric denial of it, of vulnerability, that he had not remembered always came.

He told himself: the bear isn't going to come randomly into the thick forest.

*

He sighted the young elk above the knee and waited for it to lift its head before he shot. It buckled onto its front.

The strangled ungulate blurt of its confusion coughed into the valley like some desperate blasphemy against the quietude and peace of the white snow, then was muffled as if stifled by the misted trees below.

Ston swallowed the metallic adrenaline. His spit had gone thick. He had heard the suffering and the surprise and the anger at the unfairness when he'd wounded an animal before; but it had always been an error or bad luck in the shot then, and quickly he'd shot the animal again.

He gritted his jaw against the need to kill the young elk. Not to have it alive there suffering, struggling in front of him.

*

Eventually, the yearling exhausted itself, held its broken leg bent up off the ground, with the shattered cannon bone hanging like string, and the foot lumpen.

The rope collared its head behind the juvenile nub of antler.

Some fifty metres from the trees Ston had cleared the snow from a lifted crest of ground, and the elk stood in dumb shock automatically reaching down at the green patch but not eating.

Twice the elk had gone round and tangled itself in the tether rope. Ston had gone out and untangled it. The elk stank. It stank of panic and fresh sweat, and though it only stood as high as his chest was more like a horse than he had ever known a wild animal to be.

Its breath misted out in brief, incredulous blasts. Hissed through its nose.

The bear will have eaten enough, Ston thought. Three farms. He will have filled himself and gone to sleep.

He saw his boot tracks go to and from the elk.

This is stupid.

He looked at the elk with its foreleg held in pain, nodding and not eating, and at the rope going from it off to the tree. Then he swallowed his self-disgust and shot it in the head.

Most of the day he had lain and watched.

All day he had told himself: this is stupid. The bear's gone.

*

He was still in the trees bringing out his pack and the kit to dress out the elk when he heard the *snap* like a single rifle shot.

When he came from the trees his stomach dropped.

The rope was snapped close to the knot. The air was electric with proximity.

The elk was gone, and there were huge sunken prints. The prints came from the ledge some forty metres above to Ston's left then went away up the acute slope towards a higher ridge with the drag marks and the blood and sometimes a strange scrawl left by the trailed rope like a message.

*

— It's Ston.

Hiss. Crackle.

— Anything?

Hiss.

— He's up here. He's a he. *Crackle*. He's big.

Click.

— Did you get a shot?

Crackle.

— Just prints. *Hiss.* I just got prints.

Click.

*

After the ledge the track weakened. The snow on the sun-facing flank of the higher ridge had repeatedly melted and at night refrozen and was a clouded glassy sheet.

Ston did find blood. In the softer snow, the blood looked like the bear had actually dropped handfuls of red berries. Here, it was smeared. By now it was darkening and the blood looked like oil. The bear's prints were shallow. In places, its claws had scratched up bright crests on the hard white ice.

Ahead of Ston, wind-curled drifts were piled in a maze of chambers blown down from above. The shadows made them look like entranceways into the mountain.

Ston stood in the open where he could see if anything came at him. He had reloaded the rifle with the heavy bullets after he shot the elk but he opened the breech to see the bullets there.

Ston knew the bear had gone up and over the ridge.

This is it, then. Now you don't sleep.

Now you really go after him.

*

The steam he gave off and his deep breath after the climb crystallised minutely around him in the convincing cold.

The snow had blown from the edge of the ridge and a lip of rock was exposed. Faced into the sun, the falling slope was studded with uncovered rock and juniper, and with thin dwarf trees that clung on in the warmth the bowl of the place could cosset. There were the white upward limbs of birches, and purpling alders.

Half a kilometre away, a sheer cliff rose up.

What do I do now? Ston asked himself.

It was odd to feel the solidity of the rock under his feet, after the snow's give.

Get into the thicker trees again.

Hook a seat in a tree for the night.

The thicker trees blackened, seemed visibly to regiment together as he watched. From them, a twitter of finches broke out.

The temperature had dropped hard. Ston put up his hood. With the hat too it put another barrier between him and his awareness of what was around him. He felt evident. Watched.

There was more light coming up from the snow now than down from the sky.

Get to the trees.

Having been on the stone, he seemed to rehear the crack of snow under his feet, through the hood, the hat, like muffled detonations in the sky. It sounded like the Christmas fireworks had, as he sat on the cabin stoop and heard them burst over the far-off town.

*

He found the antler at the edge of the trees. Reindeer. It was lobed. At first he thought it was a low shrub, grazed of leaves.

He pulled it from the snow. It was still attached to part of the skull. A flag of hide and skin hung from the smashed fragment.

The dense velvet scratched quietly on his thumb.

What could rip a skull?

Ston turned the antler in his hands. The hide gone to a leather rein. The tiny burrows of air in the compact bone. An obliteration.

The force was palpable.

To tear bone like that.

*

The canvas seat swung gently with his movement. He smelled fish oil as he brought the drink to his mouth, thumbed the bottle neck and felt the slight grease on the glass.

The grayling only smelled of thyme when they were very fresh. Now it was just a fish smell.

There was the quiet creak of the rope against the tree, the breath-like hush of the pines. Below, the night-greyed needles soft and thick like fur.

He took the elk dead. He waited. He didn't take it until I shot it dead. And he's taking farm stock.

He's not a driven bear. He's not driven to kill.

Farm stock and a dead elk.

He wants it easy. He's hungry. He's just hungry. He's not a mad animal.

But the strong rope? The ripped-out skull?

Will he come? Ston asked.

He had the view out from the seat hung in the trees, across the open ground and the luminous snow. Imagined the dark bear.

He's not a killer. He's not a mad bear. People have decided. People have decided what the bear is.

The drink was freezing and simultaneously heating.

It's an act. It's an *act* to believe.

He thought: I could just walk out to the bear.

The seat turned gently. There was the open white expanse of ground before Ston, and the great black expanse of late-winter sky.

He hung like bait.

How can it be possible that the bear is where I will be?

Why would the bear come to me?

He laughed silently. Why would *I* go to the bear?

Maybe the bear's only up here because I believe it is.

The clean, nasty, honest alcohol bit.

You should put your gloves back on. The cold's down. It's really coming now.

*

The fallen trees lay struck over and lain one on top of the other in a quilled line that had looked from a distance like the folded wing of a prone bird. Snow had heaped around and on the timber. The line was too long to go around.

Ston forced his boot into a gap, held a branch and levered himself on, through, amongst the branches. The deep cold had cemented his muscles. He had not eaten. He had sat in the canvas seat in the tree and rhythmically drunk the bottle.

He'd asked: Why? Why give me *those* bullets back?

They want me to hunt a bear that's just hungry and out of place but not that bastard.

He did not want to recall it.

He's trying to say it's finished. That it's over. With those bullets.

It was only when he was up on the collapsed trees, as he climbed his way over, with the spin of the night recurring and as the effort pushed the drink back up, that Ston thought bluntly: This could be his lair. He could be *in* these trees.

Then he remembered the strange certainty of the night: the bear will only be where I believe him to be.

PULSE

What if I *believe* he's in here?

The *snap* was the rifle-sound snap of the snapping rope, so that when Ston fell through the snow down into the pile of fallen trees it was as if he had been shot.

His chin hit the trunk squarely, the broken spur smashed the side of his head.

*

He woke on the snow, already inexplicably out from the trees.

His shoulder yawled. He lurched up. Spun. Blindly.

As the side of his vision went liquid, he felt it premonitionally, an imminence. That he had not understood what *had* happened, but what was about to.

His heavy pulse the footbeats of some pursuing beast.

The sing through his head the cataclysmic paw, strike, claw rip.

His mind beat backward, a bird knocked out of the air balled bleeding in a heap.

He had the gun. He still had the gun.

Run.

The body of the forest behind, giant, hunched, setting to come after him.

Ran.
   H
      e
         a
            dl
               on
                   g. Do
                        w
                            n.
                               Awa
                                   y.

*

He woke again and took a while to move.

A reddened pad of snow melted slowly in his gloved hand, palm up in the sun.

He sat up as if on a raft. Ungloved his hand and tried to pick the frozen blood out from his ear. Had an insane certainty he'd fallen from the wing of a giant bird. That he had crawled from the sticks of a nest.

The radio lay upturned on the snow with a battery gone, like a missing cartridge.

I was dragged. He must have dragged me.

When he looked up from the nearby snow to the high crest he'd come down from, the glittering stuck somehow in his eyes, crystalled the dark trees.

To go back up the severe slope was not feasible.

He fished for his inside breast pocket and as he crossed his arm over his chest to his coat zip there was some detonation deep in his shoulder. In the flash of pain, he was again hurled by the arm, dragged violently out of the trees.

His involuntary bark shocked his jaw open hard enough to jolt something in his ear and the ground swayed with the change in pressure. Sounds seeped in around his pulse.

He brought out the waterproof pouch and the trimmed-down tabs of pills. Took the paracetamol first with a mouthful of snow, then he took the codeine. Let the sugarcases soften momentarily on his tongue. Crunched more grains of snow to loosen his ear.

Looked up once more at the crest of trees.

Check the gun over. Make sure it works.

I am not going to go after you, bear. But you might want to come for me, now.

He took off his other glove and turned it inside out and with the fleece lining staunched his reopened headwound. Then he fiddled out the butterfly stitches from the waterproof pouch.

He did his best to close up the wound.

Well. He didn't tear me apart. He didn't tear me limb from limb. Maybe the pack was enough for him.

It's just a knock. It's a big knock. You got away with it.

He took an extra codeine.

He thought of the pack, with the full first-aid kit and the flares, and he thought of the broken radio. Then he thought of the bottle, even though it was empty, and thought how much he'd like a drink. He had the obscure conviction that if he had a drink he'd remember things clearly.

After a while, he didn't battle anymore with the bubble of his blocked ear. If the bear did come, he would have to see it. He likely wouldn't hear it.

If you go downhill, you'll get somewhere.

You don't properly know where you are, but.

Downhill there'll be farms. Or you'll see the town.

It's a set of terraces here, thought Ston. The trees slope, and there are flat access roads between them. Like the mountain has steps. I just have to keep going down. In a straight line.

He carried the gun uncased. He was off balance with the blocked ear and the counterweight of the rifle helped. He thought it was a good sign he had a hollow nauseous hunger.

At intervals, a high songful bell sounded in his head. It felt cartoon.

It's true, Ston thought. A bang like that. Your head truly rings.

A wind had picked up, oddly coming up from the valley floor. It brought the shush of the evergreens, the tips of which just showed above the breast of snow that fell away some kilometre ahead.

Every so often the wind rose enough to collect loose snow and whirl it like a flock of tiny white birds.

*

Ston stood at the brow. The drop was unexpectedly severe. Then he saw what looked like four table legs stuck skyward from the snow.

He went awkwardly down to the reindeer. The legs were stiffened and frozen solid. The wiry greyed hairs of the hide around the joints reminded him of his old dog's coat.

The depressions in the snow suggested a large animal had bounded to the dead animal, but there was no other sign that anything had got to the carcass.

It will take another day, by foot, to get down off the mountain. You'll need to eat.

Ston scuffed away the snow with the butt of the gun. There was powder; then, where the reindeer's initial heat had melted the snow, a refrozen shell of ice against the body.

He crazed the case of ice with the butt, knocked until it began to crack free of the haunch. Then the rifle caught.

He hit down again, again, but the butt stuck on something.

A strap.

Ston got his hand in under the leather and followed it to the buckle.

Most of the head looked perfectly preserved but the bit had cut into its mouth far enough to dislocate the jaw. The reindeer's eyes were wide open, as if it still tried to see what had happened to it.

Ston looked again at the deep depressions in the snow around.

He pictured the reindeer bolt and go over the brow, and then saw it understand the slope and its shock as it spun and thumped into the falling-away snow. Over and over, stunned.

The snorts of the other panicked animals and the surprised bear loping from the herdsman's shots.

Ston tugged the rein that taped under the snow. A fist closed round his head with the effort. He pulled with his foot braced on the reindeer's flank but the force of the set of his jaw surged in his blocked ear, then came the small clarion bells, and a firm warning pain went fluidly through his skull.

It isn't. It isn't stuck in the snow, he thought. It's attached.

The second reindeer's head was twisted backwards on its neck, and its legs were horribly broken, as if it had hit the slope face on at great speed.

Ston knelt, exhausted.

When he came to cut the meat away, he could not. There were the harnesses, the traces, the edges of the leather worn with familiarity. The buckle and clasps, the dun gold of the bullet casings. A circular halter ring with a pattern of entwined leaves.

Shoot something fresh. If you have to.

They're uncovered now. Leave these for the bear. They might keep him up here.

Surely he'll eat enough soon to go back to sleep.

Just keep going.

Down.

His headwound had begun to bleed again. He held a gloveful of snow against it and the stitches lifted. There were tiny points of light in his eyes now. A more constant ring in his ears.

These are my gifts to you, bear. For leaving me alive.

*

Once he was into the trees it was clear the stand was a preliminary strip. White stripes of snow showed between the regimented trunks and then he was out, into a narrow break.

He guessed the first line of trees had been planted as protection to the main crop that continued down the mountain, to sacrifice as a barrier if the snow slipped off the slope behind.

There are the full block plantings, he thought, and above them the sacrificial strips to hold an avalanche or deflect the storms.

It was when he turned back, as if to review this idea, that he saw the two reindeer high up in the branches.

The ripped-off leg of one was on the ground. The other hung face down, one antler gone, the skull torn open.

A chemical dizziness went through Ston as he craned his neck, and his head rang now with constant bright peals and disbelief. Then he looked away and saw the upturned runner. The elaborate, decorated bow of the sleigh curled from the drift.

A wave of nausea flooded Ston. A clean fear that this was a larder. That the bear had hung the reindeers in the trees, buried the others in the ice to keep. He was provisioning.

This is his realm, he thought.

There were heaps in the snow. Sheep-sized. Goat-sized.

Buried food.

The blood in his head thumped, the wingbeat thick in his ear.

Branches, dark feathers, lay torn from the trees about.

He clicked the safety of the rifle off, on, off, on.

He'll come back.

Then he saw the bells. A line of small brass cups strung in the treetops of the main plantation. A swathe cut through the branches as if something had ploughed into them out of the air.

*

Ston rested with his back against the beautiful sleigh. The excavated sacks around him.

The hessian was the grey of the reindeer fetlocks. The fibres glittered with rime that vapoured away under the warmth of his hand. Sometimes, the angular boxes inside stretched the sack enough for pretty parcels to show through.

One sack had burst and the presents lay strewn beneath the snow.

He unwrapped the gifts, pared back the paper as if he looked through the pages of books for some credible explanation.

Every gift he opened felt like finding a child's body again.

*

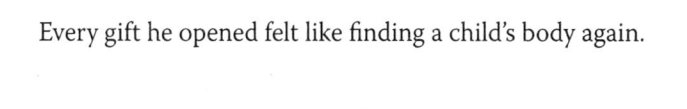

None of the toys had batteries.

He found a toolset. Confectionary. Alcohol.

The battery was in a torch.

Ston thumbed it into the radio.

Nothing. He rattled and hit the handset. Clicked the on–off dial.

A breeze swelled and rang the necklace of bells in the trees.

Click. Click. Click.

The useless radio.

It's not possible. It is not possible.

The bells like early stars.

The night was coming again. The cold coming hard.

It's in your head. You are concussed. Make a fire.

Don't go to sleep.

Eat chocolate, and burn everything.

*

As soon as he got into the truck, the acrid smell of the smoke and burnt varnish seemed to furl off him. The farmer's dog, on the back seat, repeatedly sniffed Ston's coat.

Ston stared ahead, tried to accept the disconcerting movement of the vehicle.

— It wouldn't be any trouble.

— Thank you. But just take me to the lake.

Ston's head could not go at the speed of the vehicle.

— That guy. Last year. There's a lot of us think it was right, what happened to him.

The farmer did not look at Ston. He stopped what he was saying. Like Ston, just looked out forward at the compacted track.

— Are you sure you shouldn't go to hospital? A doctor?

— It's just a knock. It looks bad, that's all. I just need a drink.

— Help yourself, the farmer said. There's a bottle in the glove compartment.

The immediate landscape blurred. The landscape beyond looked too perfect, like the scenes on the chocolate boxes.

*

— What happened? asked the police chief.

Ston saw the toys melt, the varnish blister.

— Nothing, he said. I just got it wrong. The bear's gone, I think. It's starting to melt. He'll be gone.

The police chief studied Ston. He studied the ladder of dried butterfly stitches on Ston's face.

— He wasn't a killer. He wasn't a rogue bear.

— Well.

The chief looked past the cabin. The four-day-old track cut away into the snow across the white lake.

He turned and started to unhitch the heavy Sherpa snowmobile.

— I brought rope, too. You probably have some.

In the window glass of the 4×4, Ston saw his reflection, and the scar, and out behind him the sky veiling and wrapping down on the mountains. The black definitive hem of trees cut to a flat band by cloud.

— Where's your machine?

— In a straight line up from here. She's flagged.

— I could take you up.

— No, it's fine. She'll tow.

Ston took in the square stationary solidity of the 4×4, and the Christmassy police lights. The thick blocks on the tyres and the ice compacted cleanly in amongst the pads.

— Is that a bell? the chief asked.

It was on the narrow rail of the stoop. The golden fish hung above it in a line.

— Yeah, Ston said.

Beside the cabin, the spent bed of embers lay like a dark pelt left on the snow.

— Yeah, he said. Yes. It's a bell.

Nothing seemed real.

The fish did not seem real. The track out onto the lake did not seem real. Just the bell. Just the bell seemed real.

Cow

— CLEAR.

— Clear?

— Negative.

She still held the test. Watched it as if it would change as she looked.

— Well. Then we can go, then.

— Yes.

— It was better to check.

— Yes. I thought. Really. The way I felt.

*

— Every time, he said, I think it's a lamb in a tree.

The degradable jacket hung opaque and torn in the branches. Struggled, flicked in the light wind that set across the top of the farmland.

He was trying to picture it. A lamb gently lifted up by a breeze and blown into a tree, or slipped from a bird.

The top of the ash was bare with dieback.

— Mm, she said.

He drove the lane more carefully than usual, to avoid the deeper pits the relentless rain had eaten down. Tried to imagine the old farmers he grew up around putting raincoats on an animal.

The earlies were out. Some still with their jackets on. The polythene gone clouded, like plastic drinks bottles left to the weather.

Where the quad bike and trailer had tracked up the ground, dark ribbons marred the field. The thorn was just beginning to green, and here and there gorse burst into bright yellow.

Just after the turn there was dead bracken, marked out crisp and dry when everything else was wet, strewn between the shallow runs up either side of the banks.

— They go backwards you know.

The car bounced.

— What?

He imagined her middle bounce.

— They go backwards. When they carry the bracken, the bedding.

— Shut up.

— Yes. They shuffle backwards with it.

— Shut up.

He slowed into the yard, sensed her soften, minutely let go.

When he braked, the wheels crunched briefly on the stones that had washed down the lane. The smaller the stones, the farther they'd been carried. They went in a diminishing moraine across the yard.

With the clap of the car doors, a cloud of starlings lifted off the adjacent pasture. As they scarfed away, the ground, with all the wet going through it, seemed to flitter with the sound of their wings.

There were bleats from the shed. A restful bovine low from the cattle barn. The big dun backs of the cows over the stalls.

He saw her reflect in the tight black plastic of the haystack as she went ahead, a presence in the broad round bale, then disappear into bright sheen.

Where the wrap had failed, the stack was studded with embryonic wraiths of white fungus.

When they looked over the galvanised sheet gate into the shed they saw just Da's bent back in the stall, the flank of the ewe, the pens portioned by bars of low sunlight through the slatted timber wall.

He seemed to halt a dry cough. Still bent in the stall, had sensed them, called.

— Ah! Ready for some work?

Let the cough happen.

— Bloody thing.

Could have meant the cough or the lamb he was trying to make drink.

A racing pigeon pecked at the dropped chaff on the walkway in front of the stall. Pecked flecks of straw into the air. One of its feet was only a stump. A grainy pink line.

— Where's Mam?

— She's on a sleep. Long night. Three twins and a triplet. Not problems. She just didn't get in. Tired that's all.

Then he did something funny with his throat, as if he tried to clear it discreetly.

— Calver at it, too. Big old girl.

Da nodded in the general direction of the cowshed.

— Well. Shall we take over for a bit? Do you want a break?

— No. I want to get some turned out. While we've got the weather.

— I thought it was going to rain more.

— They'll have their jackets.

The shed was full. Three solid weeks of wet, disorder had developed. There were too many lambs. They clattered up and down the wooden feed troughs that ran between the pens.

— Well. Okay. Are you tarring them?

— It's kept the foxes off so far.

He held the lamb for her, watched her eyes as she daubed the thick, creosotey tar on the lamb's hind with the old woolbag peg, then did its neck. Watched how she was.

Her eyes looked like she fiddled with small buttons.

When he lifted the lamb away from himself, the warmth stayed for a moment.

She manhandled the lamb into the jacket, legs through the holes, talked to it quietly.

With the sticky tar then the jacket on he had a thought of the lamb like one of the wrapped sweets she always had in her pockets. Somehow packaged to be edible.

— That one was big.

— That was a heavy one.

On the ground, the heavy lamb clopped its feet one then the next, then the next, then the next, as if it counted its legs after the procedure. It did two jumps on the spot, perhaps to assess the effect of the thin coat, then nuzzled the bars of the hurdle they'd penned the corner off with.

As he held the next single for her, he passively read the copy on the box of lamb jackets. *Mis-mothering is not a problem.*

He wanted to go back and check the test. Distrusted it, an unnerving certainty it would have changed the moment she'd turned her back.

The ruminant crunch, patient groans when the prone ewes shifted. Utter maternity. Inflated bags, some so huge you could think them where the unborn lambs were carried.

He watched her. Is she okay? Is she okay with all this? How could a test be more right than her body?

The *crack* of the quad bike, *rattle* trailer, *thrum* then and the sounds seemed to regroup as they came across the field.

He waited with the gate while Da backed the trailer in so that one side more or less met the warming box then he walked the gate against the other side of the trailer so that with the hatch in its back open, the trailer was the only place to go.

Thin cough.

— Who have we got?

Da looked tired of the cough. He looked tired but pent-up, to get himself over the tiredness.

— Here. Have a sweet.

She fished a handful from her pocket. Da picked one.

— That one's quite strong. Eucalyptusy.

— Good. Maybe I'll actually taste it. I had a mint earlier. Barely had any taste.

A sheep gave a cough, as if it would get a sweet of its own.

— It's probably this bloody hay.

Da kicked a discarded pad of rotted grass part-stuck to the floor.

— Mam's probably right. But. We might as well get it used.

He lifted a lamb from the makeshift keep, hung it floorwards from its front legs so the backs of its back legs dragged the ground, twisted it to see its number.

— Thirty-nine. That's the badger-face.

— She's over by the far wall.

The pigeon had come up to Da and stood by his feet, examined his wellingtons. When Da took the lamb into the pen, dangled so it kicked its trailed legs at the straw, looked tottered on tiptoe, the pigeon clobbered after him.

The badger-face looked momentarily at Da, then came up, nosed her lamb. She gave an affirmative huff and when Da carried the lamb out of the pen she followed and the pigeon came with them.

They'd lost the old terrier before Christmas, and lambing was no time to get a new dog. It was not possible to see the pigeon without the thought there'd been some swap.

Da swung the big lamb without ceremony into the wired-off section at the front of the trailer and as it scrabbled to its feet the mother went cooperatively in through the door.

— It's enough, Da.

There was not feasibly any further room.

— We can get. Or. Well. Maybe with the ground wet then.

Good.

His knee barked. He was short of breath. His fingernails burned from dragging the ewes that wouldn't go easily into the trailer. Stubborn-headed, stiff-legged refusal to step up, faces hefted in, then front feet, all their bulk slumped so he had to shunt bodily. The first one had been a fluke.

— You two want to take them? Da asked.

But he didn't. He didn't want responsibility for the trailer on the wet fields. Was offsided by the thump of his pulse after hefting the ewes. Unfit. Seven weeks since I've kicked a ball.

— I'll come, she said, bright.

She liked to see the lambs go onto the grass for the first time.

— You can do the water.

He nodded.

— And the milk, maybe, Da said. It's about right for that.

Sun lit the dust motes that passed in front of the clock.

They'll be kicking off. They'll be kicking off about now. Seven weeks. And weeks to go.

He watched her get up behind Da on the quad and hold on to him. *Cough.* Then the quad *crackracked* again, and he swung the gate to as they rattled away.

He wanted to call after her be careful, be careful on the bike.

He went to the first stall and picked out the bucket. It was misshaped with use. There was a hank of wet straw, a pinecone of dung that stained the water.

He swirled the water and sluiced it under the gate where years of the same process had eaten a shallow. Then he took the bucket to the standpipe, swilled it, and hung it on the tap.

While it filled, he half-heartedly checked the back ends, don't lamb, don't any of you lamb, for glistening strips, for lips that seemed to mutter, teeth being ground, ropes of slime. Blatant vulvas, swollen, candy pink; felt the same protective sensation as when he found pinprick sprays of blood on the underside of the toilet seat.

Collect, sluice, swill, fill. *Click* the kettle on to boil.

It could happen. It could have been positive, and we'd be in it, now. We'd be facing it.

Squeezy bottles of gloop, and iodine. Sprays. Rubber tailing rings and the applicator pliers, so the tail rots, falls away.

COW

Antiseptic wipes. A Stanley knife. Strips of coloured ear tags, the tagging gun, that punches through their ear. Syringes. Needles. Little packets. A brief wave through him. Made his balance travel. Thought of his knee, opened up, the physio saying, You wouldn't need a general. Then, of her, a cannula in the back of her hand. But it isn't happening. It's not what's happening.

Thought horribly of the ochre stain spreading in the water bucket.

Nude flesh bulged around a prolapse spoon.

The *pat pat* of the quad, coming down from the top land, the sound through the shed, then puttering onto the saturated fields at the bottom of the farm.

When the trailer was loaded again and they'd gone off with the next batch he got on with the milk. The incongruous ice cream smell of the powder formula. Two amounts into the measure cup. Added the powder to the water, swirled the jug, thought of snow, flour, cake, a child in an apron. Upended the open bottle to the inside of his wrist.

Beside him, the overflowing bin, the rolled latex of the condomy gloves, cutaway scraps of bale wrap compacted into balls. The pitch-black plastic, with the light flashed off it, one of the brightest things in the shed. Flashes of light.

— *Can you get on the floor, please, get on the floor.*

Grey when the physio lifted the injection.

— *I don't want to have to catch you.*

I won't faint. I've never fainted. It just makes me feel spinny. Like I'm on water. But I'll hold out. I won't faint.

— *Bigger boys than you have, and me five foot and a fart.*

Focus. Don't faint. Just accept it. The horrible hairline lance of the needle.

— *'Mummy,' you hear them say, then they go.*

Mummy? And he couldn't forget her telling him. Matter of fact.

— *A lot of them. Just before they fall.*

As he fed the orphan lambs, the pigeon lumbered over to the shallow under the gate and drank from the dirty puddle. He *sissed* but the bird ignored him.

Every time the bird dipped, its rainbowy neck feathers caught in the light.

He didn't feel he could get up from the lambs, tried to scuff-kick loose pebbles at the pigeon to stop it drinking the fetid water. The pink line of its leg. Saw the lambs' middles swell and tighten. Their tails flutter. Their nostrils flare with little pumps.

Heard the *pat* of the quad on its way back again. The hushed shed, the hospital sense of compromised bodies. Resting, recovering, waiting. Relegated to a purpose.

It's better. It's better we're not.

When they'd had enough, the lambs unlatched themselves, skiffing little sprays of milk up his hands. Then they shook their heads, to flick the milk drops from their muzzle, quivered, stepped back in some sort of happy shock.

He refilled the bottles, got the next orphan pair. Lifted them drumming from their stall.

Then he had the idea of the stain again spreading out in the water and couldn't watch the pigeon anymore, so he went over with the lambs infantly furious around his legs and footed the bird, which bobbed under the gate. Didn't fly. Didn't take off. It just scurried away like a little dog.

She brought the bike in onto the hard area in front of the shed and parked it out of the way.

Sitting on the bike had pushed her coat and the bodywarmer up, so when she dismounted it looked as if she had a belly.

He was raking the gouts of bad hay to the side of the aisle. Grunged pads, white with mycorrhizal net.

She came in and set the gate open.

— Where's your dad?

— He wants to get a bale in. Then check the cow. The calver.

A tine caught a raised stone in a particular way and the pitchfork sang out. Belled through the *grum* of the tractor that grundled up from the collecting yard, exaggerating through the cow barn.

A watery light washed the entrance of the shed.

— Your mum's probably right. He toed a flat pad of mouldered hay off the fork. These bales aren't good.

— Try telling him that. Did you do the feeds? she asked.

The bike had disturbed the sparrows and they were loud now in the scrub holly into which they'd fled, the far side of the shed.

— Apart from one. Wouldn't take it. The speckly one. Just didn't want it.

She was going round the shed, shining the torch at the ewes' back ends.

— Well. It's got to have something.

— I put it in the warming box.

The shed trembled with noise as Da brought the tractor in bale first. Lowered the bale to the floor and let its own weight hold it in place while he reversed and slid it off the spike. Then he came back and used the bottom edge of the spike loader to tip the bale onto its flat side.

He shouted something through the *crrormm*, put a hand to his mouth, cough, put two fingers, cow's horns, up to his head, and swung the tractor from the shed.

He was misting the stall with hypochlorite when she came back, having gone to get drinks from the house. He'd piled the barrow with neatly rolled layers of filthy straw. Blood, dung, urine.

— Da not back yet?

— No.

He heard her put the tea and coffee down on the milk shelf too hard.

A lamb knocked down the feed trough to watch him use the spray, twitched its nose at the high chemical stink. Shied as he prised the pressure valve, the *spiff* of excess air.

— Did you see your mum?

Her eyes showed briefly red in the glow of the heat bulb, then ear tags and medical things skidded, scattered as she threw up the lid of the warming box.

— Fuck's sake.

Turned, angered at him, and lurched down to lift the lamb. Like wet clothing. Pulled it. Speckled, floppy, ropey. Eyes aimless. Its stomach a concave.

— Fuck's sake.

As if it was his doing.

— Why didn't you check?

The knuckle of her little finger in the inert lamb's mouth.

— You'll have to do it.

She wasn't tender with the lamb now, held it along her legs, its throat stretched sacrificially. Loose socky rolls bunched in front of her hands, the lamb's skin too big.

I don't know what I'm doing.

— Just wait for your dad.

— We did.

There was an abrupt smatter of sparrows on the shed rafters, then they went *pinking* out through the gaps in the boarding.

— Isn't your mum coming out?

— There's Lemsip everywhere.

— What?

— Chill, or something. Throat. She wouldn't go back to bed.

— Okay, so she'll be out.

The lamb was unresponsive.

— Maybe.

— Get your dad.

— He's with the cow. He'd be back if he wasn't.

— I don't know what I'm doing.

— Just don't put it into his lungs.

He tried to *see*. Didn't look at the lamb's mouth, looked away, to some half-understood guess at its insides.

— Not in his lungs.

— I know.

— Well.

— Please.

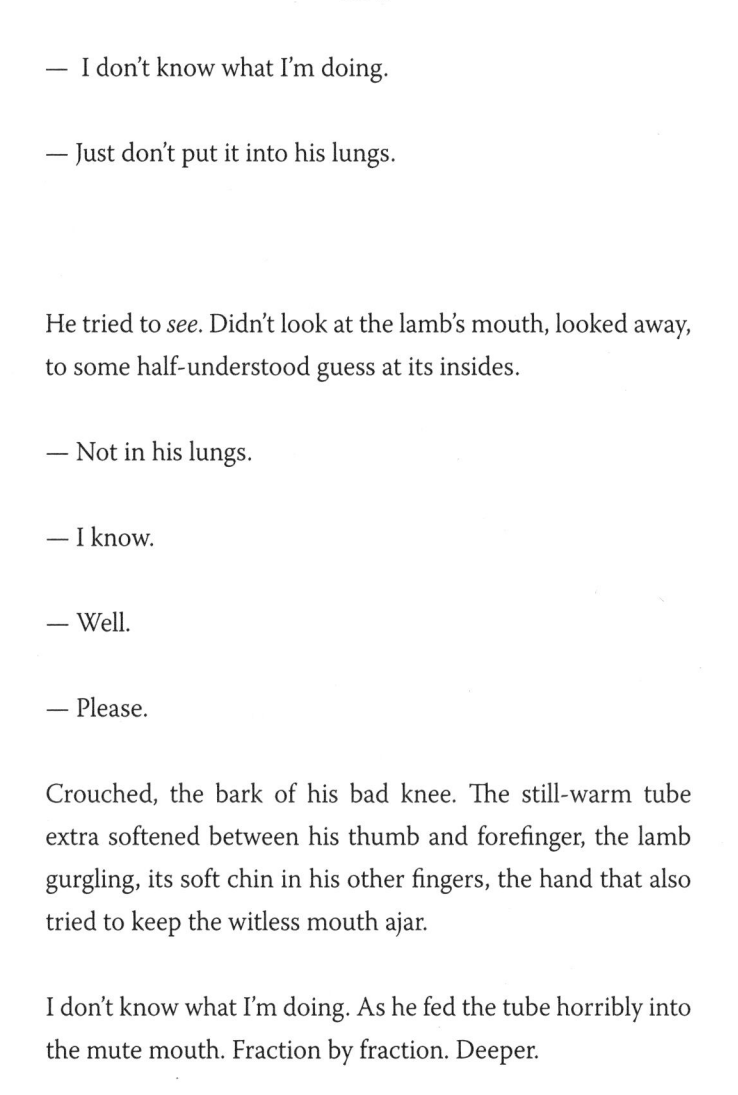

Crouched, the bark of his bad knee. The still-warm tube extra softened between his thumb and forefinger, the lamb gurgling, its soft chin in his other fingers, the hand that also tried to keep the witless mouth ajar.

I don't know what I'm doing. As he fed the tube horribly into the mute mouth. Fraction by fraction. Deeper.

Then the lamb wriggled suddenly. Christ.

— Hold it!

It coughed horribly.

— You're in his lungs.

I can't be. It would have hit the bottom of them. There would be blood. Wouldn't there? If?

Then there was a gurgle, a tight gastric stench through the tube and the lamb bridling and goggle-eyed.

— Okay, okay.

This should be calm. I should be calm to do this. Tried to fit the small funnel into the tube and reach for the milk. The world liquiding, a capsule.

— How much?

He, her, the lamb.

— Bits.

Undid the cap.

— Don't flood him. Bits. Just tiny bits.

What if I pour it scalding?

The lamb now looked alert enough to understand.

Right into it.

What if it's too hot?

He put a finger in the milk.

— That's not clean. Your hands aren't clean.

— It's fine.

— You've been doing the stalls.

— Just. Please.

She started to mutter. Started into some litany.

— Stop. Please. Stop.

Stop.

He tipped the bottle against his wrist, warm circle on his lifted pulse. The faint net of his skin, and knew she was right, saw the rime in the creases of his hands.

— You want me to use the other bottle?

The tube going into the stupefied animal.

— Do you? he snapped.

— Just. I don't know.

The lamb looked at them both.

— It's in now.

Somehow, at them both.

— Just do it then. Pinch it. Don't let it go fast into it.

He let the milk through bit by bit, tried to release, pinch. Release. Small gawps of milk sloughed through the funnel.

— More.

— Okay.

Felt the warm plugs of milk through the tube as they went down.

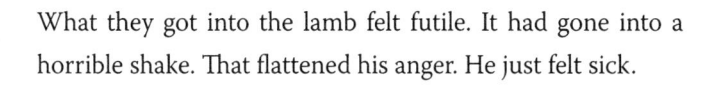

What they got into the lamb felt futile. It had gone into a horrible shake. That flattened his anger. He just felt sick.

— I'm sorry, he said.

The coffee stone cold.

— Sorry I snapped. It's. Just.

— Shall I warm that?

It's okay. That's her thank you. That's her sorry. That's her thank you.

— No, it's okay. Let's just go in. I want to do my hands properly.

Thin drools of sharp mucus brightened his skin. A stomachy smear.

— I can't believe nothing's lambing.

She tried to be light.

— It's you. It must be you.

One more check. She'll want to do one more check now. Before we go in.

— We'll do one last check.

And there'll be something.

He didn't want coffee anymore. He'd gone past it. But he wanted to go in. He nearly said, No, I want to go in. He swallowed down adrenaline. She wants to be out. She wants to be busy. It's good that we could come and help.

He watched her assess a ewe gurn and lip her teeth.

— This one doesn't look right. She doesn't look comfortable.

He had a foresense something was going to happen. He had the foresense and then her father came into the shed, finally, with the look of someone who had conceded something, and said, I've got a problem with the cow. Can you help?

*

The cow stood kept tightly upright in the bars of the crush with her neck through the pinning gate. One wet leg stuck out of the cow, the pulling rope still twisted round the calf's foot. Webbing straps went in a V from the pulling rope to the corroded bars of the run that led along the breezeblock wall into the crush. He guessed for extra leverage.

The one big leg came out wetly and slathered, the size more like something from a tree.

— She keeps slipping the other leg.

There was the one big giant leg like a saucepan handle and, barely out of her, peeped, the other. It appeared to duck protectively away when he saw it, then protruded slowly again, only the curious sensory hoof.

He didn't know properly, but to him even the one leg looked convincingly too big.

A prolonged low came from somewhere deep within the cow, didn't really leave her properly. Her dun flank bulged in the galvanised uprights. He had the horrible conviction it would be possible to saw bits off the cow. That you could saw off her legs and she'd just stand there suspended, no different, just her legs sawn away on the floor.

The yard was thick with muck the rain had corralled into piles, formed dams of, with bare channels where built-up water had rivered away through it. The boot prints behind the cow gave a record of what had already been done to try to get the calf out. Sometimes splayed boot shapes imprinted the others, looked formed with more force.

Da got his hand inside the cow and did something telescopular. Rotated the hoof out.

— Hold it.

It gave a greasy suck. Tried to slip back in as he took over the hoof from Da, got his grip around what he could only think of as the ankle, his finger joints against the rope. It was like trying to hold something thickly soaped.

— Pull. Can you get it? Get it alongside.

The white hoof, split in two sharp ovals, ogled at him, like cartoon eyes. As if they gawped in witness to the incomprehensible thing that Da then did. He climbed up on the metal run.

— Keep the leg out.

Dry cough.

Then part-balanced on the wall he stepped off the run, with all his weight, and onto the webbing straps.

The exposed leg lurched with a wet fart. The leg in his hand wanting to recoil as if the sound had scared it. Jesus!

— Keep the leg out.

The engorged udder, bulged with veins.

Da started to bounce with gentle insanity on the webbing straps. Brought a kind of ongoing *rrorl* from the cow. A bass mammalian sound amplified into something otherworldly as it resonated through the hollow metal structure of the crush. The hoof wide-eyed with surprise.

He instinctively leant back and tried to draw the hoof, the swallowed leg. The other leg, tight against the back of his hand, exposed so long it was cold. Solid. Did not feel like an animal thing.

His eyes fell to the branding on the ridiculous straps, as they went slack, tight, slack with each watery bounce. A mark on his wrist, the coat ridden up, tiny flecks of sleeve fabric patterned the sticky milk residue.

Do I speak? Do I say something? It isn't moving. I don't think it's moving.

The cow reduced to a device. The great slit of her vulva. The pronounced architecture of her pelvis.

She should be primal. She should be animate. Her imprisoned as if in punishment. As if in corrective penury.

Slap, the splatter of wet muck. Da down. *Cough*.

— Needs us both. More weight.

Get a vet. Surely. This needs a vet.

— It seems pretty big.

The cow looked gargoyled now.

Then she shouted from the edge of the collecting yard.

— Da. There's a ewe not good.

— Can't help.

— She's not right. You need to look.

She cradled the speckled lamb.

— I'm not strong enough. She's a triplet. I think they're all tangled up.

The pigeon that was now on the yard in some seeming comradeship with Da high-stepped away across the roils of muck as she came closer.

— I can't help, right now, Da called over.

— Well. I'll have to get Mam then.

— Leave Mam. Let her sleep. We don't want her ill.

They wouldn't get through lambing. They won't get through if they're ill.

— She's already up.

Da had a look. He was out of time. He'd got some lambs out onto the grass without Mam stopping him, though he knew it would rain. The bale taken in before she could argue. But he knew that once his daughter saw the cow, he would be out of time.

And then she was across the yard enough to see the leg properly, and the rigged-up straps mid-air. And the run.

Her face looked very small with all the farm clothes bunching around her and her hat pulled down.

— Da. What are you doing?

There was livid blood on the ground and around the cow's back legs now. Muck patterned in the clear shape of partial boot prints on the webbing straps.

— Dad?

Anger folding. Her face.

— What are you doing!

The leg was like some wet algae-covered limb of wood.

— You just look after the shed.

— Da. What? What are you doing? What the hell are you doing!

— We're in it now. We can't stop. We've started it now.

— I'm getting Mam.

The cow could not move. The crush held her so all she could

move was her head. She was trying to look round to see what was being done but the crush did not allow it.

Her blood was coming now in unashamed trails.

You'd have to watch. You'd have to watch this.

The cow made as if to sound a deep static noise but no sound came. It seemed to push the other sounds out of the collecting yard. She knew they were going to do it again.

— Get up. Da's eyes were flashing now.

— Da, what? Call the vet.

— It's got to come out.

Just get on it, and then it's over. It will finish, then. It will fail. And then he will have to get the vet.

— What are you doing, Da?

Just watch your knee.

When they put their weight together on the strap it was obvious to him the calf was not coming out. He was horrified the leg would snap before the calf came out.

— Fucking hell. Fuck's sake. Fucking hell.

Her shout the same time as the cow's roar.

*

He was already a metre and a half off the ground on the wall to be there to catch the calf when the vet guided it out. He had to be up on the wall not next to the vet because there wasn't much room to work with the open side of the crush so near the edge of the yard.

— *But. What about his thing?*

The vet had sent him to the shed for a bucket. He'd overheard, as he approached the shed gate.

— *His thing, with needles?*

Mam sounded hoarse, was flushed from the shouting. Puce. From the anger, the argument. The fight to call the vet.

— *Well. Da can't leave the ewe now.*

She'd been right.

— *But.*

— It's only needles. He's okay with other stuff. Blood and stuff.

Da, by the breaching ewe, didn't see him come through the gate. Spoke unknowingly.

— It has to take effect. First. He'll have done it already. He won't see it.

Dry cough. Dry cough again.

— I don't know why you brought more hay in, why did you bring more bad hay in?

Then he had to prang open the gate and they all looked up at him.

— The vet needs a bucket. Is there a clean bucket?

The vet needed it for the placenta. Did not broadcast that. The pinecone of dung leaching in the water.

He saw she still cradled the speckled lamb. Heard her as he left.

— It's just needles. He's okay with other stuff.

From his elevation, up on the wall, a sheen was on the yard. A sheen too on the slates of the old outbuildings. They looked like wet beach stones.

He looked down at the cow. The plaid shirt stretched across the vet's shoulders. The tan line on the vet's nape as he *ruzzed* the shaver over the animal's flank. Skin strange, colourless. Rich curls of fawn hair feathering to the ground.

He looked away, saw over the hedges to the green fields. To a grey ash that seemed to be singing. Then the starlings came off in a pointillist cloud; the ivy, cut, dead and hard, that roped on the trunk, like the cow's bulged veins.

When the vet ran the scalpel against the cow to score the first incision she flinched. The flank tightened like it was its own animal. She seemed to lose stability, even within the crush. She was a big cow with big bands of muscle. Deep muscle.

The vet hissed something. Inaudible. Broke into a mutter.

He could not see the vet's mouth, just the tense muscles compact at the back of his jaw.

COW

The very faint pink line in the cow's skin began to bead drops of blood. Then the vet stood from his bag with an oversized syringe, the needle in the vial.

The needle was as long as his forearm.

He felt the blocks he stood on soften.

The vet pulsed the oversized syringe, watered squirts of anaesthetic topically on the cut. A fuzz of numbness.

— I'm going to have to give her more.

Don't faint. Mummy. He'd latched on to the mummy thing as something in itself. You can't. You can't do that.

Saw a thin spray from the bright point, the vet's spread fingers on the shaved cow, actually heard the *pop* of the cow's skin.

Don't fall. You can't fall.

Do not take your eyes off.

He thought if he looked away that the world would lose anchor and he'd spin off. Into the sea of rubble and rusty metal and entangled barbed wire, the bramble, broken blocks.

He swallowed it back. Just look at it. Look. Tried to deal with it like car sickness.

Now the cow was open. Her exposed organs steamed in the cool air. Bags and bulbous insides kept slipping from the longitudinal cut that divided the cow's flank. The vet fielded them to keep them in, palmed and pushed, appeared to rearrange them somewhere inside the cow's grey middle.

A cow has four stomachs. A vet has two hands.

He still couldn't look away. It looked like the vet was trying to stop things falling out.

It was as if the vet had done something tribal to himself, with his arms and hands bright-oranged with iodine and his white apron streamed. Muttering.

— That shouldn't be there.

He waited for the wet *thwack* of something vital hitting the floor.

A cow has four stomachs. A vet has two hands. A pale blue bag palmed up and somewhere into the depths of the cow.

He felt grey, the nightmare of being horribly immobilised while somebody did this.

She doesn't feel it. She can't feel any of it.

The muscle was peeled back around the cut. Had taken repeated slicing. A line of pale hide, rim of white fat, then the thick muscle that had hampered the anaesthetic.

It looks like steak. It looks like steak. Look. You've got to keep looking. Like steak. Because it is.

There was no blood. He knew we were not filled with blood, not as if we're a bag, but to see into the cow and there being no blood made the cow less real.

The vet talked to himself. He was talking rhythmically. The muscles bulbed behind his jaw.

The cow just stared quietly out, through the gate, over the track at the fields. As if she wondered where the rest of herself had gone.

You're going to fall. You're going to fall and break something. You're going to break your neck.

He thought of the cow not feeling half her body.

Just look. Look.

It's fine. There's nothing. She isn't. It's okay. You don't have to go through it yet.

A cow has four stomachs.

The cow opened her mouth, seemed about to ask something, but instead there was a horrible, elongated wheeze. It was like she sucked in a great deep breath, to power some ear-splitting uncowlike howl. But nothing came.

The precise pink scalpel line in the very top layers of skin. The line. Pink line. Chill sweat getting colder, damped across his back.

Do not look away. The vet had the womb. The calf's bulged eyes. The uterus stretched, opaque.

The fat pink tongue lolled inside the cloudy bag, looked stunned and wounded. The tiny whorls on the calf's brow wetly printed against the membrane where it strained with the big head's weight.

The vet supported the weight, the head, a different bearing to him now, had arranged the cow how he wanted her, a vet has two hands, reached back for a knife.

Held the knife with his thumb and forefinger; precisely held the blade with the shaft under his palm and unhesitatingly drew it across the bag, amniotic water *slapped* onto the ground, a smell, the calf launching.

— Down!

As a dead weight out of the body.

He jumped. White flash from his knee, but the huge calf was there, under its own slip weight, and its head in his hands.

— Under the shoulders.

Sluiced. The protruding limb drawn back through the open cow and out to him and he carried, half-crouched, the slick weight held on his thighs to keep the calf from hitting the ground. Heard the *splotht* of the placenta into the bucket behind him.

It lay unresponsive. Its tongue lank. The leg that had protruded – it looked dislocated – stuck stiffly out and awkward.

He rubbed the calf roughly, fingered slime from its mouth,

patted at its chin. The things he'd learnt to do with lambs. Dragged the calf, the muck bunching, closer to its mother.

Clean it. Come on. Come on, even as she was being sewn up. Saw the vet's yellowed arm appear, disappear repeatedly over the ridge of the cow's back, drawing the thick black thread.

The suds in the basin of iodine, each somehow individually coloured, rainbow bubbles, the oils of the pigeon's neck.

The cow leaned as far as she could in the crush, seemed to look at the calf without interest.

She didn't feel it come from her. She didn't feel it come out.

— Lift it, the vet said from behind the cow.

The calf's upward-facing eye opened. A dark globe endlessly deep in the pure white surround.

Stain spreading in the water.

He tried to raise the inert, slipping weight of the calf. Lifted its back legs as high as he could off the ground, tried to swing the calf, to loose the fluid from its lungs; but the calf was too long. It died. It died inside her. With all his might he lifted it, arms above his head, but the calf's head still lolloped dumbly on the ground.

He began to jiggle the calf. Come on. His knee barked. Shook it like he'd empty a sack of sand. And there was a splutter. The calf coughed, and suddenly pedalled its front legs briefly. As if it tried to run into the sky. He let it down. Began to rub. Rubbed.

Come on, he begged. Come on.

Stock

HE SAT INTEGRATED amongst the felled trees, cracked a crust of bark with just the barest pressure of his foot. The rabbits, compact shapes in the field above the cottage, unfolded pointed wings and scaled into the air, as if the bark's crack had sent them up.

It was stony cold. You are sleep deprived, he told himself. Not rabbits. They were never rabbits.

The tin panged as he got up the last forkful of uncooked beans. Chewed. Assessed the tubular timber not yet fetched from the slope. The countless downed trunks.

He'd read the notice, at the edge of the devastated plantation. Some disease he couldn't pronounce. 'A legal notice has been issued to fell these trees because they are infected.' And we already have the dieback, with the ash. They're cutting them too.

What would they do? The kites now were black motifs on the nearly morning sky. If we got some big illness. Some of us. Would they cut *us* down? Cull *us*?

The TB papers. His uncle's shaking hands.

Cuckoo spit. It's cuckoo spit next. He'd seen it on the farming news. The little bugs that make it. Carrying some invasive thing. Some germ deadly to plants.

He looked around for puffs of froth on the thin growth that was coming up between the fallen larches. There's none. Too early. It's too early in the year. And then, finally, there was movement. A bar of light from the cottage.

He put the bean tin down, took the old brass telescope from his pocket. Click click, drew it to its length, raised it, unexpected chill against his eye.

Mrs Lewis Banc stood in the open doorway. With her apron on, bright and patterned, it looked like she peered over a border of small flowers.

Perhaps she sleeps in it. In a chair. Perhaps she sleeps in her clothes, like Nan.

Take them. He sent a message out to her. These are for you.

Mrs Lewis stared at the laden carrier bags before her on the path.

For you.

He sent a message out again, and now she stepped forward and bent. She picked up some food packets, held them for a moment as if they were things she didn't understand. Then she put them back, looked around, and carried the bags one by one into the house.

The door closed.

He scanned up and out beyond the cottage, to the more distant bwthyn on the hill, barely at the range of the scope, the carrier bags there just visible through the crossbars of the garden gate.

When he looked back to Mrs Lewis's cottage, he saw her framed in the window, in the lights that were on in the kitchen, seated at the table, seemingly eye to eye with a pineapple, as if the fruit were something votive.

*

The sprung bell zonged mutedly as he came into the shop, the brush of the draught baffle across the wiry mat, the snip as the latch closed to.

He carried a vaporous energy from being awake all night.

The thin plastic dust sheets that had billowed gently when the door opened settled again against the shelves.

He looked at the carrier bags still left. The goods he had apportioned up. Caught sight of himself in the glass of the Post Office counter in the corner. He didn't look the way he thought he looked.

She probably never had a pineapple that wasn't out of a tin.

He looked guilty and tired. Not as if he had done something good.

The glass-topped chest freezer gave an agitated hum. A sort of acknowledgement.

Mrs Lewis Banc.
Elin and Arwyn Cam Uchaf.
Edie Pen Cwm.
Maggie Tyddyn Llwyd.
Idris Bwlch.

They were always good to the shop. He mentally ticked them off.

The prip prip prip of postage stamps parting from their perforations. The thudunk of inking pension books.

Who else? Who else is left? Saw a map in his head.

The damping sponge, desiccated now, like a slice of stale toast.

He reached a milk from the open chiller. Jiggled it from between the cartons of fruit juice he hadn't yet shared out. Swigged. Felt a low burn in his finger creases against the cool plastic handle.

Flip-flop sound of making butter in a jar.

It's weak, this. Even the Full Fat. It's not like we had it. *The bottles achatter in the crates, the chickeny chatter of a chicken coop as Tadcu drove the van.* He still remembered the round. Which house came after which. The pull of lugging the bags in his upper arms.

He took one of the remaining old chocolate bars from beside the till, felt the till judge this act, blink, as the movement of his hand reflected in the black of its switched-off display.

Tore the wrapper with his teeth. *Taste, the glue of stamps.* The chocolate pocked with tiny nets of air, paled marks. Wildly out of date.

Took stock.

There were the few over-the-counter medicines, sanitary items that embarrassed him.

The women's refuge would take them. He felt a twisting emotional pain – but I don't know exactly where it was, where she went – through his middle, and out. And then it was as if that pain trapped momentarily in the shop as the windows hummed, a recycling van pulled up outside, idled, and there was the clatter of glass. The van just a coloured patch through the drawn net curtains.

Let it go. Let it go. Eat, now. Get some sleep. Then, it's Wednesday, go and see Nan.

Mandy. She was always good. Would come with a list for Pencarreg too.

Pencarreg's gone though. Second home. Posh gravel. Solar panels.

The nearest would be Irfon, Maen Isaf. But he has the carers, now.

He assessed what was left again, the ready-loaded bags of refrigerated goods set there in the chiller.

Everybody has to have something.

Get some sleep. You'll be out again tonight.

The recycling van gurned, rattled, pulled away. The windows briefly shook.

I could just leave him dog food. The carers wouldn't notice that. Smoothed his hand habitually across the melamine as he passed behind the shop counter, went through into the rest of the house.

*

Every time he opened the driver's door he thought the same thing. I need to WD-40 it.

He thought this time, just do it now, go in and get it and do it now, but then he thought of the hour-long drive ahead. Hour there, hour back.

He pulled the door closed, winced, even though he knew it was coming, at the arthritic creak, but more in concern it would draw attention. *The graunch of the old cowshed doors.*

He thumbed the key and the engine woke with the sort of enthusiasm of an old dog offered a walk.

It's a good engine, just the bodywork. They said it every time. Body'll go before the engine. Made the same joke every time the MOT came round, Got through on omissions. He didn't really understand it.

The hour drive there and the hour drive back, and having to drive through town, made him nervous. It was the only time, he figured, the car might get flagged by the police. But he couldn't have Nan in a nearer home, there'd be too much coming and going, people who knew her, who would talk to her, tell her.

*

— Nan.

He put the carrier bags down in the kitchenette doorway.

— Wednesday.

She looked at him, pleased, from the chair.

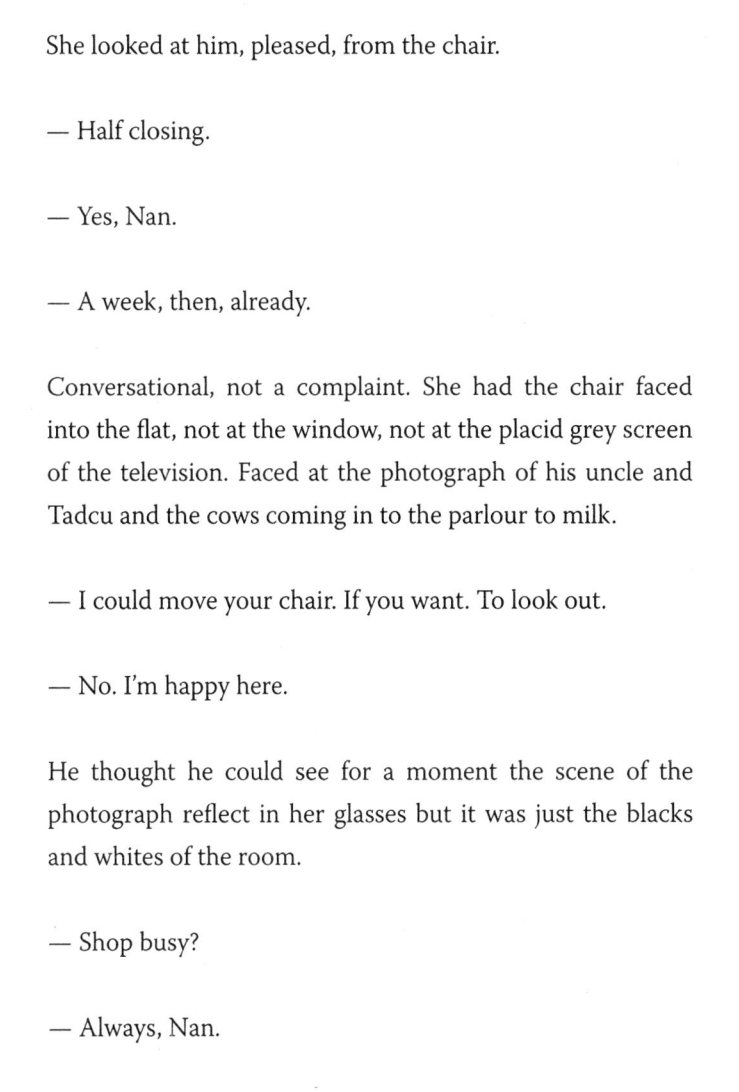

— Half closing.

— Yes, Nan.

— A week, then, already.

Conversational, not a complaint. She had the chair faced into the flat, not at the window, not at the placid grey screen of the television. Faced at the photograph of his uncle and Tadcu and the cows coming in to the parlour to milk.

— I could move your chair. If you want. To look out.

— No. I'm happy here.

He thought he could see for a moment the scene of the photograph reflect in her glasses but it was just the blacks and whites of the room.

— Shop busy?

— Always, Nan.

— Good to have the half day then.

— Yes. You can go in the day room, you know.

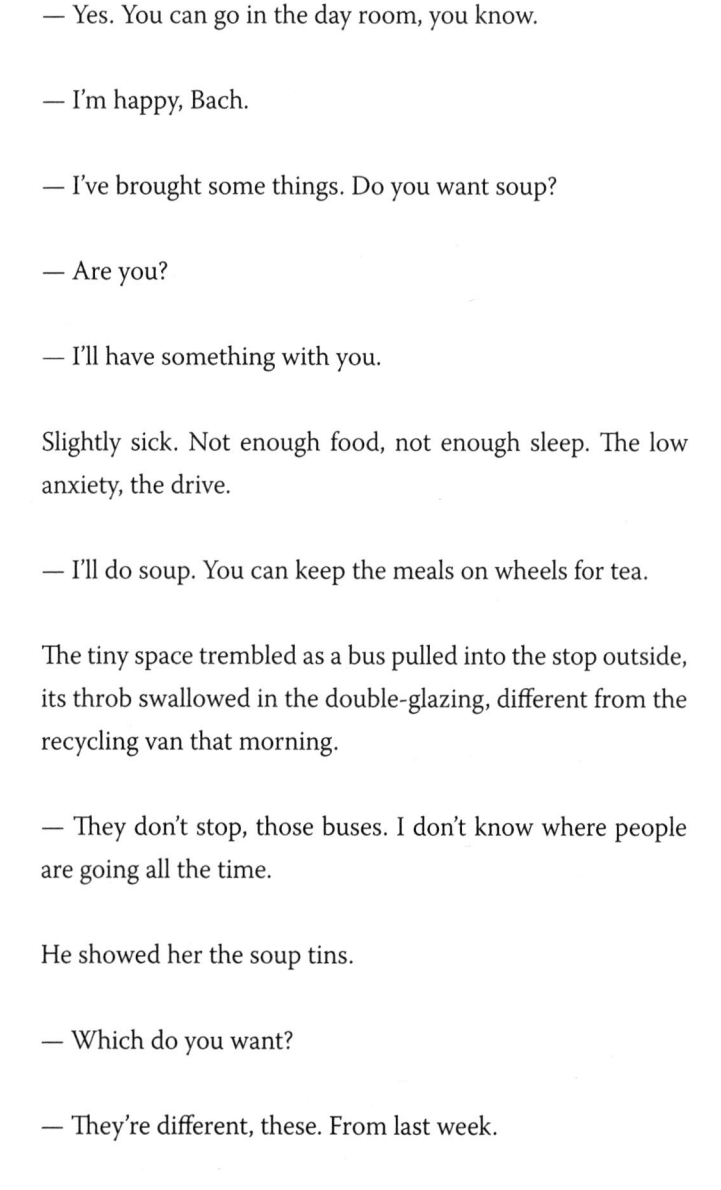

— I'm happy, Bach.

— I've brought some things. Do you want soup?

— Are you?

— I'll have something with you.

Slightly sick. Not enough food, not enough sleep. The low anxiety, the drive.

— I'll do soup. You can keep the meals on wheels for tea.

The tiny space trembled as a bus pulled into the stop outside, its throb swallowed in the double-glazing, different from the recycling van that morning.

— They don't stop, those buses. I don't know where people are going all the time.

He showed her the soup tins.

— Which do you want?

— They're different, these. From last week.

— They're the ones the suppliers had, Nan. They're the same. Just different packets.

Her hands hovered.

— This is oxtail.

— Yes.

— If you'll have some as well then.

The meaty cow smell brought a queasy churn through his stomach. He was having trouble with the smell. Already the soup was agitating in the thin pan. Began to faintly hiss.

— No Mari again today, then.

— School, Nan. I told you. She's started half days. In the holidays maybe.

He pushed the kitchenette door part-closed to get at the unit behind, fetch out bowls and small plates. Stood up too fast.

— Mrs Evans Ty'n Banc still coming in?

— Every Thursday, yes. She always asks after you.

I'm not going to be able to eat this. Grey little lumps were surfacing and turning over on themselves in the pan.

— Six she's got.

He clattered the bowls. Fumped the fridge loudly open. Put the butter on the worktop.

There was an open packet of processed ham, thin discoloured slices. A small jug of milk. He lifted the ham as a pad.

— Six!

You have to eat. Still the sick feeling. You can't be up so long, carry stuff, on nothing.

He rolled the pad and ate it, shut the fridge with a receipting suck. A fleeting remembrance of that morning in his muscles.

— Car going well still?

— Going lovely, Nan.

He thought of the perishables lined up in the shop. Lifted the soup from the electric hob. Poured it into the bowls. Found sliced bread.

He heard the soft roll of Nan's chair table as she got it in place, wheels over the inexplicable wiry carpet tiles.

— I'll do toast.

The photograph of the cows was stuck in his mind. The high hips of the Holsteins. The cowshed.

The window rumbled again as he reached spoons from the drainer, rasped the drawer open and transferred things into the cutlery tray, scraped dried missed scabs of food off with his nail.

It was the first sign. Things not washed properly. Lids not properly on the jam she made, tiny blooms of mould. These things at first he put down to her eyes.

He had a fleet, horrible thought of her being cleaned, the ladies that came. *Phop*, toast. Scraped on butter. A muted hiss as the bus moved away.

Tadcu, in the photo. Tadcu, he wouldn't have coped.

When he'd taken the food through and knew Nan would not leave the chair he took the carefully kept foil top from his jacket pocket, ran his thumb around inside the disc to slightly splay the rim.

He lifted the milk carton from the carrier bag still in the doorway and quietly took it over to the sink, slid over the cleaned glass bottle she'd put beside the draining board. Then he poured the carton milk into the pint bottle and fitted the foil top on.

He couldn't help himself glance through the kitchenette door, to Nan. To check.

Her hands were lifted slightly as she sat, fingers moving as if they worked an unseen till, but she was gazing at the picture of Tadcu, Uncle and the cows. Came back when the filled bottle clinked, as he put it into the door compartment, called through.

— There's the clean bottle for you by the sink.

— Yes, Nan. Got it, thanks. I've put a new one in the fridge.

— Uncle well?

— He's fine.

— Milk round.

— Yes, Nan. He'd like to come and see you but. He's on his own with the cows.

— Yes, he'll be busy.

— Always busy, yes.

— Always the same, with cows.

— Yes, Nan. Always the same. Everything's the same. Everything's still the same.

*

— Thank you for stopping.

— Fine, Ifan, really. Slow job on your own.

Ifan's spanned hand sunk into the fleece at the ewe's pilled haunch, pressed, read the grade of muscle.

— Still going, then.

Ifan nodded towards the car, pulled over on the verge beside the handling area, there beside the road.

— Should never have sold her!

Ifan let the ewe into the left-hand bay.

— Bargain for you there, your Nan got.

The sheep Ifan had graded so far were all in that bay. The right-hand bay was empty.

— Nineteen, *ni'n eisiau*. Why not a round twenty I don't know.

He showed the next of the forty or so ewes down the race to Ifan.

— Always fuss, with sheep. Not so much fuss, cows.

Ifan looked up and out as he pressed his hand to the new ewe, visualising the dressed-out carcass. He was looking up visualising, but it seemed he looked at the bright truck that made its way along the single-track road to the chapel clad with scaffold on the opposite hill.

— We won't have to grade them all this rate.

Ifan let the ewe also into the left-hand bay.

— Good spring.

— Not so much that. Just, I've got less animals now. Less animals on the same grass, *ti'mod?*

He nodded at Ifan. Ifan seemed to catch himself up, then.

— Sorry to mention the cows like that. Then. I didn't mean to bring your uncle up for you.

He dismissed it. As if it was nothing. Dug his grip into the next sheep's wool as she went stubborn, felt a faint rip of fleece when he hefted her.

The percussive smack of hammering came over from the chapel.

I can't really picture that, what has to be done to the inside of a chapel to make it somewhere to live in. Thought of the farmhouse. How long would it be before it was sold? Snapped up and its insides stripped out to make a country place for someone. Couldn't stop then the thought of stripped-out innards and there was nothing there, when they opened them up, no lesions, but still they had to slaughter the herd, the whole herd, after generations.

— Daughter, you too, isn't it? Ifan asked him.

He nodded again. The lichen on the breezeblock race. Splayed patches. *No signs. There were no signs, nothing on the lungs.*

— Two, see. Better, I think. Grown up now, though. I might have pushed a boy into the farm. I'm glad, *mewn ffordd*.

Ifan received the stubborn ewe.

You'll be another one. You'll work yourself into nothing and then the farm will get eaten up by a rich farm.

— This one too! There was clear pride in Ifan. No surprise mind. Been waiting three weeks to book them in.

No wonder they're grading. His nails burned from pulling at the stubborn ewe.

— What is it, two hours?

— Two hours there, yes. Bit quicker on the way back. With the trailer empty.

Two hours to the nearest slaughterhouse. Then hours more, to some supermarket butchery somewhere hundreds of miles away, to be put into packets and driven round again. Could even end up back on our doorstep.

The next sheep hovered, leant against the breezeblock channel, reluctant to move. He made some primitive noises. Clicked to her. Then he spotted her held-up foreleg.

He leant into the race to get behind the ewe, encourage her on her awkward front leg, felt the bruise in the centre of his palm again as he held his weight on the blocks.

— Bad foot, this one.

The smell of the unhealthy ewe filled his nose. He tightened his mouth as if that would close up his nostrils. Strongarmed her along. Brought a wash of tiredness up him, a loose empty feel, so when Ifan received the hurt ewe and expertly turned her over and sat her up, as if there was no effort in it at all, he couldn't connect it up, the strength.

He got over the hurdle to help hold the ewe, lifted the injured foot.

Ifan dug muck from the concave of the protruded hoof, flicked it off the clippers, bit at the big nail with the blades. Then he spread the toes. His face changed. A quiet patient revulsion.

The stink came up between the toes and out. The compact cream-coloured boil of clotted pus popped with the smallest nick, the ewe bridling as Ifan scraped a small hard node out with the clipper points and the stinking paste of rot globbed down the foot.

He turned from the stench. Turned his head away, felt oxtail bile. It was the smell. That smell. He was trying to hold away the stench of the pus, the decay. More, he was trying to hold away what was coming from it.

He looked down at his palm, pocked from the pressure of the breezeblocks. Thought guiltily of the dented shotgun stock. Maybe I could iron it out. Soak the stock and iron it.

— She's gone backwards, this one.

Ifan could tell just from handling her.

— We'll let her off.

The ewe started kicking. Pedalling into the air. Like to protest this wasn't the fate she wanted. He leant in. Tight wires of wool on her white face. A watery spit of chewed grass. Bright phlegm. There was a notch out of her ear, as if she'd already been marked out.

Ifan hissed spray onto the splayed foot, asked with his eyes down, as he checked the other feet.

— Is your uncle's barn better?

It was as if thinking about the stock had brought the question, about the borrowed gun. They'd taken his uncle's away, after.

— Yes.

He couldn't look at Ifan. Knew he was fond of the old gun.

— Thanks for the lend.

The truck had arrived now at the chapel and the delivery men were unloading a bathroom suite, setting it congregated in front of the door. The ewe's unnaturally blue one foot pointed up to them in exclamation.

— Good little gun for rats, four ten.

*

The brass scope felt different in his hands, with his skin supple from the lanolin.

He checked the time again.

She should be back. They should be back by now. Half day. She should be home.

She could have walked. If the old school was still there. An architects' office now. Same architects doing the chapel. If she didn't have to go to the big shiny new school. She could have just walked. Like I did. Or go on her bike. *Learning to ride on the yard, his uncle's hand steadying the seat.* It's a forty-five-minute run.

No point coming home, in between lifts, for a half day. You'd just have to turn around.

He picked one of last year's crab apples from the ground, shrunk and wrinkled, rolled it in his hand. Pushed distractedly against it. Thought of the puckered knuckles of the pineapple. Nan's hands. Kept his eyes on the far-off road.

It's been an hour. Since she finished. More than an hour.

Bramble was coming into leaf. Lambs bleated across the hill. There was a skylark somewhere.

They're late.

He looked at the road as if he could draw their car onto it. He was trying to hold down a sick nervous feeling. Could taste the oxtail soup.

When the car came along he found it in the scope, held it in the circle of the lens as Annie parked at the bungalow, got out, and Mari burst from her seat in the back, ran to kick her football.

A relief waved through him. Just the sight of her.

He had the strange sensation sometimes that the scope itself held Mari. That the world she existed in was *within* the scope. That he could fold the scope down, if he chose to, and carry her away with him.

But I wouldn't. I am not like that. I'd never, whatever they think.

He pushed his heels into the small ridge his feet had formed in the slope after months of him coming there. A mark of place, like the worn patch of lino beneath his chair in the kitchen, his place, ever since Mam had gone, where he'd sat since he was a child, his legs growing year by year down to the floor until they reached, as if putting down roots.

I got angry, but I could never. Not that.

He imagined the thuds of the ball against the bungalow wall, the zip of the car boot as Annie opened it, lifted out some bags for life.

Of course, he understood. That's why they're late. They'll have had to go for shopping.

Mini peppers. Cucumber. Shiny veg. He saw the list in his head. It's shiny, all that veg.

He opened the lock knife and marked in another groove. The old fence post was bleached, the greyed of the felled trunks that morning.

He was about to stand and head away, drop out of sight and follow the rill to where he'd left the car on the other side of the hill, by a slope of recently planted trees, none taller than the spiral guards around them. But as he pushed the lock tab and closed the knife, leant his weight forward a little to rise, the police car arrived at the bungalow.

Immediate sweat, a stomach churn. His palms oil as two police got from the car. What? Annie at the door before they knocked. Bones of a sudden watery, as if he was unmixing.

He hesitated as he lifted the scope, hand midway through the action, in a gesture that looked aimed to stop something. Warn.

He felt the urge to run. At the same time felt drilled into place.

She can't know. Lifted the scope. Tried to find conviction he would hear through it. She can't have seen me.

They cannot know.

A notebook flicked. A scribbled pen. Annie's ponytail shook. No. A brief scratch in the quickthorn made the sound of the pen's nib, Mari's small face, pressed at the window. No. They cannot know.

Her face right against the glass, then the big sky reflected, as if it came out of her head.

Thumps of adrenaline now.

He thought of everyone knowing. Felt fear. *Thought* of fear, the spate of raids on Post Offices, do not worry, Nan and Tadcu all those years back, *do not worry*. Shotguns. Balaclavas. Of what it would be like to be amongst the products, the shopping, and face a gun and have to really cower. To pray.

Of the police coming.

He felt sick and full of metal. Watched the police walk back to their car, open the doors, get in and drive away.

*

He met the police car as he rounded the lake. Saw the car on the opposite shore, the clean white of the turbines beyond, the low rushes stepping out into the water, two geese folded in the shallows and the sky held in the surface, Mari and the sky like her mind in the window.

Bryn Oerfa. They've been to Bryn. That's the only place up there.

He understood then. They're going house-to-house.

He slowed and pulled in. One of only a few places cars could pass on the narrow road. The gateway cut with quadbike ruts, so the car sat uneasily.

He waited. Bloomed with heat again. A slight chill immediately meeting the edges of his sweat. His neck vein thick, suddenly. Too small.

The worst rusted side won't show. Not how the car is in the gateway like this. They won't look, he told himself. That's not what they're doing, here. They've got better things to do than notice an old car.

The other car neared at a steady, measured pace. As if it didn't want to spook him.

Sit. It's just panic. A fish in his chest. Remember what the doctor said. Say thank you. Thank you, body, for warning me, but it's okay. It's nothing. It is not a lion.

For an insane moment he believed he would spin the car around, flee, or ram the police into the water. Take off on foot.

How would they find me? Dogs? It would be the only way. A hammer percussion in his chest.

But they can't know. Calm yourself. They cannot know yet what it is I am doing.

He looked through the gateway, at the ruts that continued away into the field, a track that had been set.

Briefly, the police car was out of sight behind a lobe in the road, and then it reappeared, slowed, the police waved him an acknowledgement, and passed on with a nod.

*

He got only a few metres before he had to stop the car again, the horrible graunch of the car door, *the cowshed door*, got out and was sick. Hands on knees. Biled. A two-tone slug of goose shit. Blue condom wrapper in the grass. A burst of feathers, closely scattered, fallout of some bird taken as prey.

When the sing of endorphin died back, the air thumped with the turbines, the beat on the breeze from the far ridge, *thwock thwock*, an under-roar that fell into time with his decelerating pulse.

And then he laughed – you mad bastard! Delightedly. You're mad. You're cracked. They do not know. Midges whined above his vomit. Obviously. They do not know – was still laughing when he had to get back in the car and reverse out of the way of a smart people carrier, a family, so he guessed, coming for a stay in the lovely countryside.

*

He held his hands in the cool edge of the river, flexed his fingers. They looked abnormally white in the tan water. The red marks of the carrier bags disappeared.

He was still and engrossed in his hands.

When he looked up, birds had come to drink at a shallow beach across the way. Orange-red, or green-yellow. They were birds he'd never seen before, and in the strange liminal state that early in the morning, they did not seem quite real. They dipped, lifted, tiny clicks, made subdued *djeeps*, the sound of a squeezy dog toy.

When he moved, the birds scattered.

The contained *cuff* of the falls filled the place. Glassy peals of broken water.

There was no green at all on the oaks, tight closed on the steep sides of the gorge. Still late to open.

I'll get up high, through them. Up to the top to see the road.

Birdsong had burst the quietness of the woodland as he'd followed the cwm down. One lone bird, then myriad, as if in praise of him. Less a chorus, more a drumming, an incantation.

By the time he reached the falls, perhaps only because of the previous ceremonial intensity of the song, it had come to feel strangely quiet.

That's something they made fun of, when I was little. He

used to think the sun rose because the birds called to it, sang it up.

No one disabused him. Then he went to school.

It's merciless, school. They tell you it's training for life, but it's not. It's not anything like life.

He studied how his skin looked unnatural in the water, closed his sore hand on a submerged stone that fitted as if designed into his palm. It looked an amphibious colour. Surprised him when it wasn't slick. Take it with you. He lifted it.

Use a stone this time.

His hands were icy. He shook the water from them, then dried them on the woollen balaclava.

The resin the water had not washed off his skin tacked to the fibres. There was that and the lanolin oils from handling the sheep.

The sweat of manhandling the fallen tree hung damp now in his T-shirt. A cold patch under his jumper, stuck against his back.

What are you doing?

The eyeholes of the balaclava seemed just then to gawp at him. Ask disbelief.

No. You do this. It must be done. People need to see. That if things don't stop everything will just be gone, will go. And we will not get it back.

Even the pubs have gone. Chapels. Now the schools.

The little shop.

No.

Stop.

A shiver went through him. A reset.

The orange-red and green-yellow birds had come back. Djeeped. Supplicating to the water.

Everybody on the list. Everybody who helped the shop. Everyone who was kind. Everyone who misses Nan.

Stop.

Don't fall into that angry thing, now. Get it done.

He picked up the bag. The birds scattered again. He looked up through the oaks.

Get done what you have told yourself you are going to do.

*

A crisp green salad and shell-on prawns.

He kept the supermarket delivery van centred in the scope. It seemed to stall almost, to make the awkward turn up and on to Ffosffin.

It's like a toy. It's like a toy van. It's like a happy little van on children's telly.

The cardboard box under the stairs, with the fire engine, the taxi, racing cars, and the plastic trucks, people figures bigger than vehicles, out of size, giants.

He read the inane cheery claim on the boxy back of the van, watched as the vehicle throttled down on the lane, took the bend, passed the handling area, Ifan's sheep, and went out of sight.

*

STOCK

Ten minutes at Ffosffin with the delivery. They unload the shopping into a wheelbarrow and take it back and forth. Then a few minutes to loop back down the lane to the road.

He'd dropped down off the rise, through the geometric plantation, the soft-cushioned underfoot needled floor, followed the little spots of marker-spray on the trunks to the loose tree he'd left balanced in the early hours.

He strained to listen through the passive *hush* the breeze put through the conifers.

Nothing. Not yet.

Then, little *djeeps* broke the hush, *djeep djeep*, the birds, them, now again, busy, drew his eye to see frail tawny flakes helicoptering around him, nipped from the cones they busied at, *tiny upside-down pineapples.*

He put out a hand but the flake he aimed to catch sailed from the movement, displaced like a small object in water.

And as the flake found the ground, he heard the van.

Its specific motor sound amplified in its tinny carcass.

Yes.

The birds broke away as he moved, his weight against the levered tree, so barely held, spun, so that with one roll, a hard bite into his shoulder and with a creak more metalish than timber the trunk lurched off the slope, snapped an artilleral *crack* as it met the tarmac surface, reared once, and fell still. As the motor sound developed, tone-change, lowered gurn as the van geared down in anticipation. Just around the corner.

He rolled the balaclava, raised the gun, and stepped into the road.

*

When he lifted his hands from the steering wheel, they tacked slightly.

He turned off the engine and, for a moment, there was an intense peace.

He unhooked his left foot from under the seat, stretched it in the space he'd expect to find the clutch.

He took a breath. A moment. Prodded the vehicle tracking device like you might a small dead animal, to check it was really dead. Felt the sharp upturned lip in the plastic where he'd smashed the lock knife in, this time with the river stone.

Squeezed his fingers into a fist to feel what he thought almost was yesterday's deserved dull pain in the centre of his hand.

Then he got out and graunched shut the cowshed door, and the place fell into dimness.

It made the other delivery van that was there seem to lurk.

It held him, unnervingly, as he let his eyes adjust. Then he went back to the van he'd just parked, and reached the .410 from the footwell. Perhaps sensing him, the man locked in the goods bay of the van began desperately to shout.

He steeled himself, put back on the balaclava, threateningly bashed the concertinaed side.

— Enough. I'm going to open the hatch. Don't say anything.

The roller side crattled up. The driver was on his knees, gripping the shelves as if the van was still travelling.

— Out.

The driver gripped the shelves like to let go of them would cause him to fall. Like he would drop.

— Out.

He kicked down the foldable step.

In some daze, the driver moved, slowly climbed out. The thickened rubber soles of his shoes looked remedial. Toyish, like the van itself.

The driver was cramped and shaking. His lip jabbered. When he saw the other van, a pathetic sob went through him.

— There's no money.

— Have any people bought freezer bags?

The driver didn't understand.

— Someone's bought freezer bags?

They had. Several people had.

— All the stuff with the supermarket name on. Go crate by crate. Anything in a packet with the supermarket on. Take it out. Take it out of the packaging and put it into freezer bags. If they are tins and things you can't do that with put them to one side.

The thick lenses of the driver's glasses went briefly opaque.

That's what happens. It's what happens at the moment an animal dies. Its eyes go out.

He raised the shotgun. Felt the pattern of the wool in his skin as he pressed the stock to his cheek.

— Please.

— Crate by crate. Separate everything out.

He couldn't smell the cowshed through the balaclava. Just the damp clothes smell. He couldn't feel the dryness of the cowshed. He was sweating. His hands slick on the gun.

There was the sweat, and the grease of the lanolin, and the resin tack, and the starch effect of the grain, from when he'd swapped out the lead from the cartridges.

It was nearly done.

— Not the bottled water. Keep some toilet roll.

The driver was on his knees amongst the boxes. Packaging strewn, blatant. The driver's childish thickened upturned soles.

— Tuna. Do you like tuna?

Tight dapples of light came now through the clustered holes the shot had made in the galvanised wall behind the chair when his uncle pulled the trigger. Bright solid pellets.

He tried to block the thought out.

Tried to unhear the detail, the flies. He shouldn't know. The holes. He couldn't dislodge the thought they'd eaten through the wall. To get at him.

Stop.

— Tuna.

A discarded bakery item bag uncurled on the floor, as if of its own accord. As if it would unravel and scuttle across the cowshed floor.

The driver looked incoherent. Again a sob, more a choke, came up.

He checked the own-brand cans to see they had ring pulls. Bananas. A bag of already chopped carrots. Own-brand sliced loaf.

— Jam?

The driver was crying now. Full-on crying.

— Do you want jam?

He passed in the torch and brought down the roller side.

There was a sudden silence in the cowshed.

The hair on his nape stiffened.

It felt the silence came profoundly from, was generated actually by, the other van.

He gazed at the re-sorted goods. Re-bagged meat, grey through thin blue plastic. The discarded packaging across the ground, *strewn feathers from a taken bird*. Slim scattered straw. A desiccated pellet of cow cake, *goose shit*.

And then a sobbing broke out from the latest van by which he still stood. A sort of bovine moan. Then a sudden din. A crazy batter. Like the clang of a loose gate. A noise that cracked at his skull. The white bonnet. *White police car*, a sudden compression, overtaking, doubt buzzed. The horrible flies.

— Enough!

The light through the holes in the wall fell in rods, white tunnels of dust.

— Enough!

The deep silence came back. Again seemed to come from the other van.

He went over. Approached as if the van would shy, or bolt, kick out like an unnerved animal.

Why is he so quiet? He was mad yesterday, he raged.

He patted the roller door with the butt of the shotgun. Nothing. Sailed for a moment on a horrible soupy uncertainty. Tried to secure himself to the ground. Then he undid the latch, *it's not a lion*, barrels levelled as the door scaled up.

The stink of shit and urine hit him. Came through his uncovered mouth, came as taste.

The driver squatted crouched on the diminished case of sparkling water bottles. He'd more or less demolished the inside of the bay. Gouged where he'd tried with the frames of the racks to lever away the side panels. His hands cut.

STOCK

Blood dried on the van floor. Crusted on his uniform.

He looked so slight, even in the tiny goods bay. His body contorted between the mangled lengths of angled metal.

Just stared, the driver. Stared at the gun. Looked back at him with blank disgust.

He relowered the door. Lifted off the balaclava. Everything was spinning now. Try to get a hold. It's choice. It's a choice. You've done this.

Everyone on the list. You have to do everyone on the list. If nothing more.

Thought of Nan. Thought of the wiry carpet tiles, the blunt nose of the struggling ewe. Tried to grip some detail from the day to hold to. Like the doctor'd said. Green-yellow birds. The bags. The stacks. Taken stock. Boxes all around the floor.

But the cowshed was alternately compressing, shrinking and expanding, chasmic. The walls.

He looked up at the spattered holes, the tight dots of light. *They ate him. They came in and ate him.*

— What do we do now? What are you going to do now?

The driver's shouted question echoed in the van. Contained. Words clattered. Flies.

— What now?

In his head. Little holes.

— What happens?

Burst out.

Spinning.

— What?

Spinning.

— What happens now?

White Squares

THE PELLET STRUCK the duck on the side of its head and it seemed to jitter momentarily then fell sideways in the water and came to rest against the stones in a shallow part of the stream.

He could not help the feeling of surprise that the other ducks hadn't lifted and flown. They just proceeded on.

They went past where he was on the riverbank and from behind he saw their tails lift and dip on the current of the water. It looked like their tails were having a conversation with one another.

He shot another in the back and it seemed not to notice for a while but then sank partially, eventually tipped, and floated away upturned with the rest.

He knew it was unlikely a next shot would hit a duck forcefully enough.

— Pigeon? He figured if it would take pigeon it would be enough for the ducks.

— It will take pigeon, the man said. Decent shot. Pheasant with a headshot.

The gunshop owner had the build of the stock of a gun. When he looked at you it was like he was assessing your readiness to have a gun. He had the manner of a man who had a responsibility in giving you a gun or the things that went with a gun and did not seem to be delighted by the act of sale. Like if you got it wrong it would all come back on him.

— Pheasants are stupid though, he said. Most of the time they don't know they've been killed. You'd need a good headshot. Even then they'll likely run around. You have a dog? he asked.

— I don't.

He'd bought the air rifle and the tins of pellets, one tin of them with pointed heads which he thought would be more effective for the duck on the water. When he opened the tin to look at the pellets the smell took him straight back. How his father and he shot at old plastic bottles in the back garden on the estate and how he had rested the barrel of the air rifle on the windowsill, kneeling on the back of the sofa inside because he was too small to hold the weight of the gun.

When he paid the man for the gun he told himself the money should be going straight to the boy, or really to her for the boy. But he was still angry at the court. He'd had no intention of not paying towards his son no matter whose fault it was. He was angry actually *at* the court – the physical object of it itself, as a person can be angry with a low doorframe they walk their own head into. The statements that had been made seemed to him part of the court itself, and the way she'd said, He never does anything, he never gets anything done.

He knew it and he was dismayed himself, but with the gun on the back seat he knew he would show her. He would do this thing for the boy.

He got a way downstream of the ducks and waited. He'd made a run through the growth alongside the river so that he could head down it without hindrance and keep constantly ahead of them. He did not believe in God, or did not admit to belief in Him, but he was thankful the river wasn't so full. The last few Mays now had been near starvation dry for the grass and the early vegetables. In the concave cuts earlier spates had made in the riverbank the tree roots looked parched grey, and it had been so dry and the river so low for such a while that the small stones studding the riverside clay were working loose as the earth tightened.

At first he stood with the barrel of the airgun rested on the arm of a smooth thin beech that grew in the bank in a lanky way as if it had shot up from too much river water the way a teenager suddenly bolts up just on eating crisps. He could not imagine the boy as a teenager like that. He could imagine him as a man but not as a teenager all elbows and neck. He could imagine him as a man perhaps because that was abstract; but his being a teenager was very close and in some ways too close round the corner to imagine.

He felt restricted standing and in a strange way not illicit enough, so he lay on the bank as he had before with the little tin of pellets in reach of his hand. He thought of how he coveted his father's tobacco tins as a child and how he was concerned when his father left as to where further tins would come from. That thought had gone round and round in his head as his father was crying walking out after hugging him, the way the silverfish he caught went round and round the inside of the tins.

You don't see silverfish anymore. They were just a given then. The bathroom, in the cracks of the floor tiles. You didn't have to think about them being there.

He thought, ashamed, of shooting the finished cans off the top of the fridge from ten foot, hunched up against the far wall of the bedsit. A whole tin of blunt pellets bar one which he rolled round and round the indented trough at the bottom of the tin until it was just a silver blur. The pellets bedding into the plasterboard wall behind the cans like the stones in the soil of the riverbank.

He recognised he was thinking about silverfish running round the inside of a tobacco tin and not about the ducks and feared for a moment the ducks had gone past though he knew they had not. He scolded himself to concentrate but could not shake the weird sense of his father crying and that night after he had gone; they'd had garlic bread from the freezer and laying down now there was the earth smell and leftover scent of the gone-over wild garlic on the bank.

You can't rely on luck. The luck the boy was having was all bad. He thought of how the boy's face would be if something in all this bad luck went right.

When they appeared round the curve in the river there were a few fewer ducks, as if some of them had taken flight in the interval.

His first shot missed. They were at some distance and it was ambitious to shoot them face on. They were a smaller target that way but he hit the lead duck in the chest then. It jumped up and slapped clumsily back, skeeted into a quick run of water. He fumbled for a pellet, cracked the gun and loaded and had to tell himself to calm down. He missed again with the second shot at it but the duck then seemed of its own will to concede and just went to rest stuck in the fingers of a snapped branch that had fallen into the river.

Can't get anything done he said to himself, and he knew generally that was the way of things and believed it the way eventually between all women and men. But he was going to get this done. He was confused for a moment whether the image he had was of himself watching his father cry or whether it was of his boy watching him.

He shot the next three ducks angrily and they tipped and went away in the stream. Ludicrous as he knew it was, each time he hit one of the ducks he expected the others to startle and fly up from the water, barking and out through the narrow channel of trees.

*

The boy was with the rest of the school on the harbour when the one duck came down the river. It seemed the harbour itself sucked in with a collective anticipation waiting for other ducks to appear, but they did not.

The children broke into a quacking at the surprise of the first duck appearing, unrecognising yet there were no others, and the one teacher in his waders in the water by the white rope decorated with little pennants the classes had made gave a sort of bemused peer up the river.

There was a crowd of parents and others along the side of the harbour so it looked like an overgrown bank. Whether there were any more ducks coming or not, it was clear the one single duck was way ahead and would win and there would be no exciting race between ducks at the ending as there had been last year, the little huddle of them spinning and wobbering in the mini currents and his boy's falling uselessly back and back and eventually grounding itself without even finishing. Some people always win things. Other people never win anything. The face the boy had on him then was something he couldn't get from his mind.

She was there a little way into the crowd behind the boy and he wondered whether the distance he had to keep away remained the same if there was a body of water in between.

White squares had appeared now in the hands across the harbour as if the crowd were waving handkerchiefs to the incoming duck. The white squares each had a number and that number could be worth a thousand pounds but he knew as he watched from the opposite side that only 43 was worth anything and his boy had that in his hand.

He drove off before the teacher retrieved the single lone duck with the net. He wanted to imagine the boy being close to him when it happened, not see it from a distance.

As he drove away there was the clunky jostling of the sack of ducks he'd managed to pick up at the shallower points from the river and the tinny rattle of the tin of pellets in the car doorwell; and as he hung a moment before taking the junction out of town he recalled perfectly the sharp high smell that came from burning plastic. The warped shrunk bottles that they'd shot melting down in the garden fire. How his father had moved the bottles further and further away each time he hit one. How he'd at last been allowed to shoot targets on a small white square of paper.

Pulse

HE FOOTED OFF his shoes, the logs balanced on an arm, and tugged the door shut. Behind him the rain slanted into the open porch in tight, rattling crescendos. Pulsed with the crashing wind.

— It's foul out there, he called, but she wasn't in the main room.

He saw the signs of water ingress in the planks below the cabin windows. A wet stain that caught the light. Every autumn. Every autumn, he thought, we say we'll seal the planks. She'd put towels down where the rain had been driven in.

When he stepped from the doormat onto the wooden floor he felt the damp sock under his left big toe, the result of prising off the right shoe. With the wind baffled by the walls, the spat of the rain seemed even louder as it thrashed the low metal roof.

She'll be trying to get the little one down for an afternoon nap. That's why she hasn't responded. The little one whom they hadn't expected to have – the child who was at once a present fundamental fact but, even though she was walking now, and talking, still bewildering.

He went into the middle room, knelt by the wood burner, and set the logs down, placing them loosely around the fireguard, trying not to knock them together loudly, even though that wouldn't be heard above the weather.

Tiny drops of wet mist silvered his jumper.

I should have put a coat on. The wool won't dry properly.

Two weeks. Nearly two weeks we've been waiting. No heating. Still no engineer.

It was wearing. If they wanted hot water they had to use the kettle or heat up a pan on the hob.

He went into the little one's bedroom, keeping the arm he'd used for the logs forearm-up so specks of wood and torn bark wouldn't fall on the carpeted floor. There she was, asleep, despite the storm.

His wife was standing at the window. He could see the

concerned set of her, the tightened curve of the tensed muscles behind her jaw.

— What is it? he asked.

Her eyes were fixed on the high stand of pines at the edge of the lawn. They whipped and flailed. One of the heavier pines seemed to be leaning into the crown of the thick cypress in front of it, a few metres from the cabin. The thick, furred cypress seemed animate, wallowed in some conflict with the pine, as if it were trying to hold the other tree back.

— It's come over, she said.

— It's just the wind.

— No, the tree's tipped. It's near the lines.

Three high-voltage cables passed overhead, between the line of trees and the cabin. They'd had them assessed. A surveyor had come out and done checks, explained the readings, confirmed that there was less emittance from the lines than a microwave could give off. The surveyor said whatever hum she could hear, it wasn't from the lines.

He watched the tree. The power lines that seemed to vibrate tightly in the gale. The branches lashing.

Years back, on one of the local farms, a line had come down on a wet field full of cattle. The farmer had to watch, wait, for the electricity to be switched off. A worker from the power company had to get to the substation and shut it off by hand. Meanwhile the animals filled with electricity, some of them immolating, burning up then in the wet field.

That was decades back. The system was different now. Centralised. It would cut out immediately.

A *thwack*, rattle, as a stick hit and rolled across the ridge of the roof.

There were sticks all over the lawn. Ripped whips of evergreen, bare staves of dismantled ash. Torn leaves stuck to the windows.

As the light fell, the cabin seemed encased in a translucent shell. The world through the windows melting repeatedly, running into pools of itself. Remaking. Running again.

Sporadically, the crack of a thorn log from the wood burner broke through the grey noise of the storm; the gurgle of rain choked the guttering, overspilling in silvery beads that *spacked* against the cabin planks.

He found it abstractly peaceful. The little one rapt in headphones, the window nearest the television glowing and colouring with the reflection of her cartoon on the glass.

He was sure the wind was dropping, that the rain had begun to abate.

And then his wife came back from the window where she'd been settled, watching the pine. As if to keep watch would stop something happening.

— It's definitely moved.

He looked down. The floor was busy with farm toys, frozen mid-event.

— It will just knock the power off. If it hits the lines, the power will cut.

He looked out uncertainly at the soaking-wet lawn.

— Anyway, the pine won't hit the lines. It can't get through the cypress.

He looked at the tide lines of bright clutter all about the place. Lines pushed by the waves of play – the disarrayed plastic farm animals, a black-and-white cow.

Rain sprayed the windows.

It was like being in an ark.

— It's like being in an ark, isn't it?

He raised his voice for the little one to hear through the sound of the television in her headphones.

— What's an ark?

It won't hit the wires.

The lights in the cabin dimmed then, for a fraction of a second.

The pine was leaning farther into the cypress. It looked now not as if it were grasping stupidly, furiously at the out-of-reach power lines with the fine-needled tips of its branches. It looked now to be reaching intently toward them, with one long curled stretch.

He tried to look up at the lines.

He knew without turning that she was back at the window.

He felt an unwanted stonelike sensation that, with everything else in motion, the whole world made fluid, she was the only still thing, the middle of the gyre, around which the calamity whirled.

He looked back then.

His daughter had her eyes right on him, watching him, as the flecks came down through the sky and the rain hacked into the ground.

The storm will blow itself out. Surely. It's going to blow itself out.

In the main room, rainwater seeped between the joins below the window frame, gathered momentarily on the upper edges of the thick, angled planks, then ran down to the floor. The tea towel she'd set there was sopping.

— It's coming into her bedroom, too.

— Yes.

— It's wetted the carpet.

— I know.

It didn't used to come in. It didn't used to get through. There's just so much force now, in the weather.

He looked at the black clouds of mould on the double doors that led onto the lawn.

— You never did the sealant.

— I know.

— I bought it ages ago.

Water seeped through the panels in the doors, too.

She let the door of the sink unit slam.

— Where are the candles? They're always in there. Why aren't they?

If they send people out they'll just butcher the ground, he thought. It'll just be butchered. There'll be Land Rovers and trucks. The lane will be ruined. For one branch. It's just one branch.

— I'm going to put her down.

— Okay. I'll just go out and check things. I'll get more logs.

I'll get it done. I'll just get it done, and it will take the worry off.

It's just one main branch.

For a moment the space within the porch felt taut, like a chest full of air – it had the pressured imminence of held breath. Then the gust dropped.

It was exhilarating, to step out. There was a sort of abandon, stepping into the storm.

He coiled the lengths of rope he'd picked up over time at the nearby beach, the salt-bleached cords almost friable, impossibly dry in the small shell of the woodshed.

It's one branch.

No one will come out to deal with it in this.

A small, compacted wasp clung to the fibres of the blue rope, drawn in on itself, in some suspended sleep. It was possible to believe only that some outside agency had stilled the wasp. It was not possible to believe that the thing had cast itself into that state.

It seemed completely abstract with the storm raging all around.

He loosened the wasp, teased it out using the frayed end of the rope with a sort of care, and let it drop into a gap in the woodpile.

He moved the axe. He caught sight of the telescopic polesaw. The ladder rapped against the roof as a rail of wind came in.

It's just one branch.

If he looked up, the rain drove into his eyes and sawdust dropped onto his face. The air gurned.

Each time the wind snatched the sail of the upper branches, the thin blade of the polesaw bounced on the branch. He had no control with his arm upstretched – this is stupid, what am I doing? This is stupid – tidal lurches lifting through his body. And then the ladder skidded slightly, the saw blade twisting stuck in the branch, the pole slipping from his hand to hang out of reach midair. And he thought he was down. A sickening creak – he thought he would go – as the ladder lost purchase on the wet bark and bit into the beach rope that held it fast.

His stomach dropped. Seemed to spin out into the wind and he just hugged the mast of the tree as everything tossed and broke and waved, his sodden face pressed into the skin of the trunk, and his head filling with a reptilian hiss.

He felt a pure, infantile fear. The smell of pencils. The cold metal smell of the ladder. There was a static crackle above him. And it froze his blood. His body filled with a heavy ice.

A *c-cr-crackle* again. The pole of the saw like some clock weight, swinging.

It flashed into his mind to leap, to hurl himself into the swell of the cypress. But he could not move.

You're on a metal ladder.

He stared out. *Crackle*. His eyes dropped to the field beyond, the molehills like compact heaps of ash.

Move.

He could not look up. Move. He could not look down. In the storm light the ladder glowed against the waterlogged pine. The air rasped.

Fall. Just get off the ladder.

From deep inside the tree, he heard – he felt – a primitive, arrhythmic beat. A slow basal drumming.

Crackle.

Down. Get down.

He lowered a foot – gave up agency to the tree itself that coached him – another foot. By foot. Feet that fluttered in the chasmic moments of the depthless blank space between the rungs.

As he passed the rope he'd tied to bind the ladder to the tree, he smelled salt, the white stains of brine washed out around the trunk. A fizz to it. A tiny wildness. The sea of the storm. The crash of the wind. And above, in the dim light now, again the static crackle, like some failing radio device. A percussion of crisp sharp electrical clicks.

Down, a primal thump in the heart of the tree again, down, toward the swirling pit of the ground.

— Call someone.

— I did. I have, she said. What were you thinking? What were you doing?

The resin would not come off his hands, the side of his face.

The rain had stopped, and against the saturated dark wet of everything the assessor, passing purposely among the trees in a white helmet and hi-vis jacket, looked like one of the little one's toy builder figures.

There was sparse light left now.

It had been an hour since the storm had lost force. Abated. But the air seemed laden, held a sense it was not done.

Fat drops *fonked* onto the cabin's roof, fell heavily from the surrounding trees; the lane ran with rills of water, deepening channels in the softened mud.

— I'll go out.

He stepped into his boots and pulled up the waterproof trousers he'd left attached around them.

— It's better if I go out.

— You tried to go up it?

The assessor's question was accusatory.

Seeing the ladder against the trunk now, he recognised how big the tree really was. How short the ladder was against the thick pine.

The polesaw swung above them. Negligible.

— Yes.

— Hear those clicks?

Crisp taps in the air.

— That's arcing. That's electricity jumping from the wires.

A sort of motion sickness came over him.

— Two metres that current can jump. At least.

Again, the ground seemed to lose its certainty. An illusion – just the wind, pushing through the cluster of bramble at the foot of the trees – exaggerated as the fluid wake of adrenaline went through him.

Then he saw that the ground was actually moving. The earth around the pines lifting. It seemed to swell and exhale deep within the briar. To pulse as the wind swayed the high trees.

In the crepuscular light, each tree trunk seemed to be growing from some breathing, harboured animal.

The assessor walked past the tilted pine and stopped at the neighbouring tree. He watched the pad of its base lift, the root ball loosened in the soaked ground, the weight of the mast pitching in the wind. Then he went off, kicking through the bramble as if it disgusted him, already on his phone.

— It's a switch-off. I don't need to see it, I can hear it. I'll give you the pole numbers.

It was dark by the time the three trucks from the power company came up the lane, and from the cabin they saw the beams of the lights swirl and scan in the field beyond the line of pines.

The wind was lessening all the time now. It had lessened, but still it gusted. Gusts that landed thick and heavy.

He thought of the lane. The mash of it, with the fat tyres of the heavy vehicles, the wet ground at the field gateway.

When the tree surgeons saw the ladder – as they came into the line of pines, with head torches and handheld floodlights, voices loud over the wind, swearing as they went into the bramble and the overgrowth – twice he heard the word. Twice he heard them say 'hero'.

The little one flinched when the *carack* of two chainsaws ripped out, looked about to wake. But she stirred only, adjusting her position on the sofa cushions they'd laid down as a bed in the middle room. With the electricity off, in the light of the fire, she looked not softened but smaller and more serious.

The quick throttles of the saws told him that they were

cutting away the bramble, the spurs, ridding the area of the thin thorn first.

The wind was a low hiss. It gave the sense it was circling the place, an uneasy beast stalking a clearing, at the centre of which was the pine. As if the pine were some quarry that it wanted to rush, and take down.

Everything seemed unreal in the whiteness of the floodlights.

He watched the tree surgeons. The groundman and the climber, and two younger-looking lads who were clearing the brash, every so often looking nervously at the swaying tree and the lifting bubble of the ground around its trunk. He saw the climber kick his foot spikes into the trunk and lean back into his rope. Saw him flick the looser second loop higher up the trunk with a quick, snapped action and then lean out again into the tension of the line as the groundman below him took in the slack.

Above them, the polesaw hung, still bitten into the tree, swinging in the wind, knocking against the trunk. Dull, redundant thuds, jeered by the bright metallic clinks of the climber's gear.

Thunk. The climber kicked his spikes into the trunk. Stepped.

Flicked the first loop over the second. Leaned. *Thunk.* Stepped.

When he came level with the ropes that bound the ladder to the tree, the climber took a pruning saw from a scabbard at his waist and cut them. The ladder came down.

Thunk. Spike.

The climber climbed slowly, rhythmically. The only break in his rhythm came when he stopped to remove a broken spur, a partial branch, the awkward side shoots that disrupted his route up the thick trunk.

As he climbed, he seemed to be further quelling the wind. It was his pace, the controlled process, as if he were some sort of handler.

When he got to the branch, the climber wrested the blade of the polesaw from it and let the saw drop. He secured himself, and began to rearrange his clips.

The rain that blew from the branches caught the mesh of his visor, made the visor look like some medieval face guard.

— It's moving, the climber said. And then, in Welsh, *Mae'n symud digon*.

The others were just standing watching now. Watching him get set.

He was right at the edge of the light that welled up from the work floods, the pine reaching away into the dark above him, his chainsaw slung from a short rope off his belt.

When he swung the climbing rope up toward the next strong branch his eyes followed the throw, the beam of his head torch cutting a bar like a searchlight, illuminating bright gems of resin on the bark, making the moisture the wind blew from the surrounding trees shine like diamond spits of rain.

Then the beam settled on the wet grasping arm of the branch that reached for the wires. Circled in compact, fluid loops of light with the uneasy movement of the tree.

He was thinking of the wasp. He could not move it from his mind. The strange sense that had emanated from it, motionless, in the lash of the storm.

The chainsaw kicked in then. Raw, gruelling yowls, splitting in short, saurian bursts amid the fall and crash of dropped branches. A clang, sometimes, from the ladder, as it became more and more buried.

The gap in the line of pines was blatant. The air smelled of resin, of spent fuel.

On the ground, the severed branch looked oversized. Looked so big now it was down.

A truck started up, and over the small belling sounds of the climbing gear being packed away he heard the ground mash under the vehicle as it turned in the field, briefly lit the trees in silhouette, and then slushed through the field gateway, spattering onto the lane and away past the cabin.

The groundman looked at his watch.

— Should get you back on now. Won't be long. They want us to do it within an hour. Sixty minutes. We get fined otherwise.

It seemed that cutting off the branch had stopped the storm. It was strangely quiet.

— Do you want tea? Something? he asked the groundman.

We can make tea on the gas.

Away from the felled timber, the climber got out of his harnesses. Stepped out of the straps and belts.

On the ground he seemed oddly proportioned. Two-thirds leg. He looked tall and thin and very strong.

He took off his helmet.

Without the helmet, he seemed older. He didn't look as if he had come down fully from the tree.

Another of the trucks started up. It spun briefly on the wet field, then got onto the lane, and he saw the two younger tree surgeons as they drove past, white-faced in the light that was on in the cab.

The climber sat on the high stool in the cabin. He was tall enough that he had to extend his legs out and away from the stool. The groundman was on a chair at the kitchen table.

She'd found candles, and everything was softly lit.

— Sugar?

— Three. *Diolch*. Thank you.

Three.

There was not a fleck of fat on the climber. His hands, which were resting on the worktop, looked astonishingly strong but not thickened up like a farmer's might be, or blistered and dirty; there was no visible middle age around his jaw, his cheeks.

His very pale blue eyes moved slowly around the cabin, as if he were waiting for something to pass, or to leave him.

He was looking at the construction. At how the logs fitted one onto the other.

The pan sissed as she lifted it from the gas hob and poured the boiled water.

— Ta. *Diolch*. He lifted the tea immediately, his hand around the hot cup, and took a sip.

It's the sugar. He wants the sugar. He's in a sort of self-controlled shock.

The groundman, too, was looking around at the cabin.

— Lot down tonight.

— People don't manage them is the thing, the climber said.

He saw his wife watch the climber take a measured mouthful of tea. Controlled.

She looked flushed. Her pupils widened in the candlelight.

— New storms, see. Twenty-year storms all the time now. With the climate, said the groundman.

Then the climber spoke.

— You'll have to sort the others. Those other pines. They'll all be over.

Her question came, a glance at him.

— Once you get one, like that, they'll all go. If they're planted together in a stand like that. If they've grown together for years, and one goes over.

He couldn't help but think of his grandparents. How they'd died within weeks of each other.

The climber seemed momentarily distant again. He took another measured sip of the tea.

— It's not the trees that go. It's the ground.

Then the lights blazed on. The cooker clock. And the television box whirred.

By the early hours, there was barely a murmur.

A soft sheet of wind. A sense of fatigued relief.

The electrical noise of the house. Quiet, persistent. Over-present.

After the tempest, it was unnerving.

Since the child had been born, sleep was like some sort of raft he just had to climb onto. But tonight it lapped away beyond reach on his ebbing adrenaline.

He got up from the pullout bed where most nights now he slept, threw on the waterproofs and coat over his sleeping clothes, and went outside.

With the wind dropped, in the light from the porch the lawn looked brushed as if with some deliberate care.

The lopped-off branches of the pine were heaped around the foot of the trunk, the several yards of the tree left standing thick and scaled in the beam of his torch. Great flanks of cut cypress lay lividly green in among the dropped brash.

The field beyond was marred with dark tracks. The ground at the gateway mutilated.

He turned the torch back to the sprawled offcut. The sheer quantity of foliage he would have to clear up. The springy, wrinkled cables of pine. The spiked, needled brush. The sectioned heavier boughs.

There was a sense of murder, of an attack that had passed.

In the remaining trunk, the climbing spikes had made repeated triangular cuts, like bite marks in an animal's neck.

*

He angled the branch into the drum, thick end first, and the branch bucked and sprung as if it consciously flinched from the spinning blades. More than a week had passed since the storm while they waited for a woodchipper to come available.

He pushed the branch deeper, until the blades themselves chewed the remaining length through. Bent again for another from the pile he'd so far dragged to the gate.

He felt strangely detached in his earmuffs, the white chips loosing from the chute and escaping out onto the gateway that was all turned to mud.

The heavier chips had flown farther from the machine, taken through the air by their own weight. Then there were progressively smaller chunks. The patch closest to the chipper was little more than sawdust, floured around by the slightest breeze.

He pressed the red Off button, pushed the earmuffs to his neck. Listened to the declining spin of the blades as the residual energy went from them. Took off his gloves. They were sticky with resin, the marks like those a sticking plaster would leave on your skin.

He looked at the piled branches and offcuts by the fence. The stuff he could chop into logs he'd put to one side.

He'd barely made a difference to the mess around the tree. He hadn't even done enough to free the polesaw from the cut-away brash.

You just have to keep going. You just have to keep going until it's done.

Late in the afternoon, he noticed the floury sawdust blow back across the machine. Settle on his sleeve, his fleece. The wind had swung.

He took off the earmuffs. Looked up at the high line of trees. Noticed, overhead, a countless crowd of seagulls cutting inland steadily.

No one had come to tend to the other pines. No one could come for weeks. Everyone with a chainsaw licence was clearing the wind strikes and the fall from the storm.

And then, from somewhere, the memory rose. The rabbit burrow they'd dug into last summer, while trenching the potatoes. The curved shallow run they'd found within the soil. The collapsed earth dropping and rising, seeming to lift with the rhythm of breathing. He'd felt a primeval disquiet, some anciently imprinted caution that he had to breach, and then a protean jolt when the thing moved, when he saw the black globular eye of the exposed kit, itself some hole, the entrance to some compact endless tunnel.

An unnerve welled in his stomach. A slow whelm like the ground moving, the slow rock of the trees.

It's the ground. We just have to hope that the ground holds.

He went to their bedroom, looked in on the little one, asleep, small on the double bed.

He remembered how he'd stood like this, watching her sleep, just after the electricity had been turned back on following the storm. And then he'd seen what he thought must be the tree surgeons' torches, flashes of light that played across the window. He'd moved the curtain to one side and seen a cackle of small lightning lick up around the ceramic insulators on the power lines, blaze around the top of the pole that carried the wires.

He remembered how the dizzying fear had hit him, as he ran out to the groundman and the climber, who were walking back to their truck. The water rilling in the lane. The lips of the churned mud. How he'd called, It's lighting up, it's lighting up. It's sparking. And how the groundman had just said, It's the salt. From the wind. It's burning off the salt.

He looked at the little one now for a long while, listening to her strong, purposeful breaths and the sea sound of the air shifting the pines. He heard the wind picking up, intensifying again. From the same direction the last storm had come.

He looked at his wife as she came in, at the expression he'd seen in her eyes before, on a plane during the dropping thump of turbulence, at the thick dressing gown she wore, the pelt that covered the hot-water bottle in her hands.

— Shall I lift her into the cot?

He could tell before she answered. He understood, because he, too, felt that the little one had become, to each of them separately, their most safe point. That if they were within reach of her breath the rest of the world went away. Nothing more mattered, not even each other.

I miss you, he wanted to say. I miss you beyond any means I have of coping with the distance you have gone.

— I'll go on the pullout. It's fine, he said.

He shut his eyes. He expected to see again the bright, white wires of electricity playing through the dark. But all he saw was his child, asleep under her blankets, her eyes moving quickly below the thin lids, as if she looked out at some incoming weather front.

*

Her scream smashed him from sleep. Her scream and a wakening to a flash so total there were no shadows, her skin and the little one's skin bright electric white, her screaming his name, then a pitch blackness, a shotgun blast, and again the light, and her screaming, It's down, there's another one down, it's down on the line.

— It's come down. It's come down on the lines.

As he lifted the little one, the flash came again, and a searing crash. A haptic infrasound through their bodies. *Zrum*. Then again. Then again. Light. Three times, the snatched glimpse of them so forcefully burned into his eyes that he thought he'd been killed each time, that he had grabbed that look at them just before he burst into flame.

— Get out. It's over the roof. Get out!

The air was like the sea. The storm alive. Stepping off the porch like leaving a boat, into the deep crashing water.

If the power's in the ground. If the force is in the wet ground.

The cattle, catching fire. His tiny child in his arms.

Acknowledgements

THANKS TO JOHN Freeman, without whose call I wouldn't have written *Cow*. Thanks to Cressida Leyshon at *The New Yorker*. Thanks to Laura and to Euan.

Thanks also to Nicholas Royle, Michael Hingston, John Norton, Duncan Minshull and Kirsti Bohata, and to everyone who's been in my corner over the time these stories have come to be.